PENNY MAYBE

BY KATHLEEN MARTIN

Penny Maybe

Kathleen Martin

Published by Kathleen Martin, 2024.

Published by
R. McDuffie Publishing

First Published by Second Story Press
720 Bathurst Street
Suite 301
Toronto, Ontario, Canada
M5S 2R4

PENNY MAYBE

First edition. May 2, 2024.

Copyright © 2024 Kathleen Martin.

ISBN: 979-8224852338

Written by Kathleen Martin.

For Adam and Jim

ACKNOWLEDGEMENTS

My thanks to Isabell Simpson, Patricia Parker, Dianne Garrels, Charis Wahl, Linda Steiger, Jennifer Wood, Martha Fusca, Ashley Isaacs-Trotman, Rhea Nicholas and Kathleen Vaughan, and to the Canada Council for the Arts and the Ontario Arts Council.

The physics question on page 27 is taken from *Matter and Energy: The Foundations of Modern Physics* by James H. MacLachlan, K.G. McNeill and John M. Bell (Toronto: Clarke, Irwin and Company Ltd., 1963). Reprinted with permission of Stoddart Publishing Co. Ltd.

Chapter One

"You can't get drown in Lac Ontario
So long you stay on shore."
- French-Canadian chanty, 1885

The idea of swimming Lake Ontario came to me after I split up with Chester, my boyfriend. Well, he's not really my boyfriend, not in the traditional sense. We had never dated or anything like that. I had never even looked him in the eye – I was too afraid to – but I loved him as much as my battered heart could love anyone.

I just kept imagining that one day something would happen that would force me to face him: like we would be trapped in a stalled elevator, and there would be nothing left to do but start a relationship because it would take a few days to be rescued. And by that time, we would be so together that nothing could pry us apart. But what really happed was I saw him at the back of McDonald's, where he worked part-time, kissing a girl on the neck.

My name is Penny – not the short version of Penelope – just plain old one-cent Penny. My last name is Maybe. It isn't my real last name. It's a name I chose because I am never really sure of anything or anyone, especially myself.

Planning to swim Lake Ontario wasn't the first time I'd thought of some way-out way to deal with life's kicks in the head. When my parents took off just after my seventh birthday, I decided to teach myself how to fly. I would fly away from all the pain and into our solar system and into solar systems beyond ours, without the aid of anything but my skinny little arms – one of which broke after I jumped out of my bedroom window.

I don't know why my parents had me in the first place. Parenthood was like a hobby to them to be put aside when it got too bothersome. They fed and clothed me but only until I was able to do that for myself.

They bought me lots of toys- anything I wanted. They would have bought me a pony and let me keep it in my room if it could have kept me occupied and away from them.

Sometimes I would creep downstairs and hide behind the living-room curtains, so I could be close to them. Discussions ran like an electrical current between them, white-hot and crackly. I desperately wanted some of that current sent my way. Sometimes the desperation got too desperate. I would be drawn to them like that foolish moth to a flame, only to be told I would be happier with someone my own age and sent back to my room.

They both died in a car crash. They were probably paying more attention to each other than to the road.

Chapter Two

In a book I got from the library, I read that Lake Ontario is 271 metres deep, 288 kilometers long, and 85 kilometers wide.

My bedroom now is 3 metres deep, 3 metres long, and 3.6 metres wide. Lake Ontario is approximately 15,000 years old – 14,984 years older than me. I know that comparing me and my bedroom to Lake Ontario is like comparing a pencil to a computer, but I still find it an interesting exercise. And no matter how much older the Lake is than me, it was sixteen years old at one time; and no matter how big the Lake is, it might not be big enough to hold all that is in me that I don't want anymore. The problem is, every time I think I know what is in me that I want to lose, something happens that won't let me let it go.

I wonder if Lake Ontario feels pain the way I do. We are polluting it like crazy. At least I can run away. It can only lie there and take it. Maybe the only way it can get back at us is to throw up big storms and drown as many of us as it can. Maybe it's waiting to drown me. Maybe I'm just going crazy. But so are my current foster parents. Their names are Helen and Dan Norman.

At first, I thought I had finally hit the foster-parent jackpot. They gave me the only thing foster kids treasure: a room of their own to hide in.

I had to share a room in all my other foster homes. I had to bunk in with some strange kid who thought I was even stranger and who hated the idea of sharing her or his parents. It was sibling rivalry without the "sibling" part.

The most difficult roommate I ever had, however, wasn't a kid. It was a primeval grandmother who kept hanging onto life a lot longer than necessary. She lived in the first foster home I was in. We not only shared the same room, but we also had to share the same bed. Halfway through every night, she would wake me up and moan for a bedpan, which I had to install and empty.

One morning I awoke to see her parched eyes fixed on me. Her mouth was open like a rigid "O," like something had surprised her, and a thin brown line of spit ran down from it, across her pillow, and onto mine. She was stiff, and cold, and dead.

I had a hard time sleeping in that bed afterward. I had a hard time sleeping anywhere. I started sneaking out at night. It was the only way I could get any sleep. I would lie down on a bench next to a busy street. I found the traffic racket comforting. It would lull me to sleep.

My first foster parents didn't approve of how I dealt with insomnia. They thought I was on my way to or had arrived at being a prostitute. I soon found myself back at the foster kid depot.

"Can I have my own room?" was the first thing I asked at the next foster home, and the next one, and the next one after that – there's been so many they'd make a large suburb. But the answer was always a variation on the theme No. One FP told me that I should be grateful to be in a room at all, that there were tribes in Africa that left unwanted children in the jungle to fend for themselves, and I was super lucky to be born in Canada.

That was pretty confusing. I had come from a "tribe" like that right here in Canada – my parents. I wish they had put me in a jungle in Africa. I might have had safer experiences. I might have had more interesting experiences. I might have become the female version of Jungle Boy.

It was different with the Normans. Seconds after I arrived, before I even asked for it, Dan said, "We have a room just for you. We have it all fixed up. Wanna see it?"

He transformed right before my eyes when he said that. He went from being just a regular guy, with more than a hint of a beer belly, to looking like Jesus Christ with his heart exposed.

Helen was entirely different. Her heart wasn't exposed. It was layered in diamond-hard ice, the way I hope my heart would be someday.

"Don't get too attached to your room," she said. "We first have to get to know each other and see how things work out. There's no sense in rushing things."

She was right about the room. I didn't want to get attached to anything again. I believe I knew that right after they cut my umbilical cord.

"Well, let's get to know each other then," said Dan. "Whadda ya like to eat?"

"How could what a person eat tell you anything about them?" asked Helen. "Besides, I'm not running a restaurant here. I'm sure she'll do just fine with what we like to eat."

It was time to start my usual bullshit. "You're right, Mrs. Norman," I said. "I'll eat just about anything. Thank you." The "thank you" came out as smooth as milk.

"We don't eat just *anything* here," she said. "We eat good food.'

"She's a great cook," Dan added. I could tell he was trying to lighten things up, but Helen controlled the dimmer switch.

"Do you like school?" she asked.

"Mrs. Norman," I replied, "I'm not like most kids my age, which take for granted the opportunity to be educated." I was now using my I-have-a-big-vocabulary voice. It always made an impression on foster parents. "I treasure being able to go to school more than anything else." I might have gone over the top with that one. Even I had my lying limits. I felt a sudden itch on my face. A new pimple was about to be born.

"Well, Mrs. Horshaw, your social worker, told me you were having difficulties at school, "she said.

"It's only because I've been relocated so many times," I answered. "But once I'm settled, it takes me no time at all to get caught up." I was a cunning vixen. I could get out of anything.

"Yes, I suppose all that moving around was the problem," said Helen.

"Wanna see your room?" asked Dan before Helen could take another bite.

Bless you, Dan, I said to myself. And your sacred heart with its underlying beer belly.

Helen led me up to my room. I held my breath as long as it took to get there. It was a habit I had picked up to calm myself when I got too excited about anything. I made it to the door. Helen opened it. And there it was: my first very own room in eight years.

It's strange. My first bedroom had been like a jail cell, but this one was like an escape to freedom.

"Dinner will be ready in an hour."

"Thank you, Mrs. Norman," I said, then added a little more buttering. "Do you need any help with anything?"

"You'll be expected to do the dishes."

"No problem."

"And don't use that expression. Mr. Norman uses it constantly, and I find it quite irritating."

"I won't ever again. Thank you, Mrs. Norman. Thank you."

"You might as well just call me Helen. I think that would be a positive first step, don't you?"

At last a little drop of melted water had fallen from old ice heart.

"Sure, Helen. Thank you."

"And I wish you would stop saying *thank you*. If I have to put with Dan's *No problems'* and your *thank you's*, I'll go crazy.

"Yes, Helen, I'll try not to," I gave her my practiced smile, the one I reserved for foster parents. She finally left me alone. "Thank you, Helen, you mother-fucking bitch," I whispered politely as I closed my bedroom door.

My room had a dresser, a night table, and a single bed, none of which had any particular style. The space was like a big empty page. The first thing I did was write *Penny was here* with my blue ballpoint pen, in very small letters, behind the headboard of my bed. Then I unpacked my bags and put away my wardrobe of twin clothing: two pairs of jeans, two T-shirts, two skirts, two blouses, two pairs of panties, two pairs of socks, two bras (which I didn't need), two jackets – and one dress.

Afterward, I sat down on the bed and stared at my two jackets and one dress hanging in the closet without anyone else's clothes next to them. I savored the feeling for as long as I could allow myself to, and then put everything back in my suitcase. As Helen said, "No sense in rushing things." I tried to rub my note out with a wet finger, but it turned into a blue smudge with its own thing to say.

I forgot to tell you that the dresser had a mirror. I try to avoid mirrors because I can't help looking into them.

I always have the same reaction. The eyes that stare back at me look as if they belong to someone else. They never express what I'm feeling inside.

The technical part about them is that they're brown like an orangutan's. My hair is like an orangutan's too. Straight and coppery. I hope the comparisons stop there.

"Everything okay?" Dan called through my closed bedroom door.

"Yes, fine."

"Hope you're hungry, cuz dinner's ready."

"Great, I'll be down in a sec." I got back into bullshit mode and headed downstairs.

Dan was at the head of the dining-room table, hacking off a big slab of roast beef.

Helen sat at the other end, spooning roast potatoes onto her plate. They looked like they were in two separate worlds.

"Want the end piece?" Dad asked, waving a slice of meat impaled on a fork. "That's my favorite."

"No, thank you. I prefer the middle part," I said, not wanting to deprive Dan of anything. Then I suddenly remembered I had slipped out a forbidden *thank-you*. I glanced at Helen, but she was too busy choosing the perfect roast potato.

I wasn't the least bit hungry. My stomach felt swollen with gas. I wanted to let go with a huge fart, but the Normans would need gas masks. I forced the food down. Each bite tasted like wet Kleenex.

"Mrs. Horshaw told us your parents were killed in an automobile accident," said Helen, like it meant as much to her as if my pet slug had been killed. "How fortunate you weren't in the car with them."

"Yes," I replied. "It's one of the many blessings I have to be thankful for."

"But how unfortunate that you've been through so many foster homes." She stabbed a roast potato with her fork. "I was a foster child myself, but, unlike you, I stayed with my one and only set of foster parents right up until the time I could take care of myself. Of course, they took proper care of me when I was little. I guess I was lucky. It's too bad the system failed you, but you can't blame the system."

"I'm just completely grateful that there is any kind of system. It's just one of –"

"The many blessings I have to be thankful for,'" Dan said, mimicking my bullshit. "You've gotta pretty grown-up way of talking. You always talk that way?"

"Do you always talk that way," said Helen, correcting him.

"Yep, I always talk this way," Dan replied with a teasing smile. Helen glared back at him, but he held onto his smile. "What's for dessert?"

"Dan, she hasn't even finished her dinner."

I thought I had, but when I glanced down, the food I had eaten had somehow managed to reappear on my plate. I thought about sneaking some of it into my pockets, but Helen had her radar turned in to my every movement.

"Looks ta me like she's had enough dinner for one night," Dan said, picking up my half-finished plate, for which I was eternally grateful. "There's a TV in the den if ya wanna watch it. Or you can just goof off up in your room.

Whatever you want."

After making sucking noises through her teeth, Helen gave in with a quick nod.

I backed out of my room, bowing like a servant, and ran upstairs to my bedroom so I could start breathing again.

Chapter Three

The Normans' house is a two-story redbrick box. It's typical of every house within a radius of at least fifteen kilometres. The front door is dead centre with a concrete porch topped by an aluminum awning supported by four twisted metal poles. Two windows on either side of the porch stare back at you with aluminum awnings shielding them like half-closed eyelids. The roof meets like a pointed cap over it all. It all looked to me like a giant face buried up to its mouth, doomed to suffocate forever.

Inside the house, Helen keeps everything operating room clean; even a microscopic bug couldn't find a microscopic crumb in it to survive on. All the furnishing had been carefully chosen for their complete lack of any style to call their own: they're neither tasteful nor tasteless, they made no statement whatsoever. It all adds up to the absolutely nothing look. There are no knickknacks, or pictures, patterns, or plants (alive or simulated), frills or curls, or even a slightly wavy line to interrupt the monotony.

***

I wonder how long I would last in Lake Ontario? One day it's hard enough just to open my eyes. The next day I'm planning to swim Lake Ontario. But my brain has always worked that way: black or white, up or down with no in-between. My goal is to live in an in-between state of nothingness, the capital of which is the Normans' house.

I decided to list the top ten things I would have to do to swim the Lake, but I could only think of two: 1) become a better swimmer, 2) find a coach.

The swimming part I can handle. I learned how at my second foster home. It was with the Jamison's, an older couple that lived on the shores of Lake Simcoe. Mrs. Jamison taught me how to swim because it made her too nervous about sending me outside with "All the water so close by just waiting to drown a little girl like you."

Mrs. Jamison warned me about so many things. If my secret last name is Maybe, hers must be Never. She would say, "never play on the road cuz if you get hit by a car, I'll have to scrape your brains off the asphalt with a spatula and never pat any stray dogs, cause they're sure to have rabies, and if they bite you, you'll die a screamin', mouth-foamin' death."

Mr. Jamison used to take me fishing because the Jamison's' other two foster kids, both boys, were afraid of deep water and refused to be taught how to swim. I told the boys I wasn't afraid of anything. Of course, that made them terrorize me. They would put praying mantises on my head when I was trying to read and grass snakes in my bed when I was trying to sleep. Once, they put a snake's head in my cereal. I've never been able to eat Cheerios since.

"Did I ever tell you how hard life was before I met Mrs. Jamison?" That was always Mr. Jamison's' opening line after casting his fishing line into the water. It was always the same story, so I can quote it verbatim: "I used to ride in boxcars across the country with a whole bunch of other losers. We'd jump off whenever we got to a place that looked like it might have jobs, but there were always railroad police waiting around to catch us.

I remember one guy got his legs sliced off by a train when he was chased by one of 'em. He ended up bleeding to death. I ended up in Vancouver, the most beautiful city in the whole world, course it's the only city I ever was in."

"I got a job washing cars. That's where I met Bonnie. Back then, she was a great gal who laughed like a horse. We moved back to Toronto cuz I hate mountains and I ain't never looked back since."

After telling the story, he would open up a large case of beer. "What a lucky man I am," he would say after the first beer. "Every day, I get up and just count my blessings on what the Lord has seen fit to give me."

But it would always end up the same. By the time he had drunk his way through the case, he would talk a lot differently about his life. He'd say it was "Jesus-fuckin' awful," and he would fling the empty beer bottles over the side of the boat, and they would float around us like little brown bodies. Then he would pass out, and I'd have to start the motor up and hope to find the way home.

One time the motor wouldn't start, primarily because it was out of gas. There weren't any oars since Mrs. Jamison kept them to whack her carpets clean. And there weren't any life jackets because Mr. Jamison thought they were for sissies.

I decided that the shore didn't look that far away, and I could probably swim to it. I slipped over the board and started swimming.

I learned something that day about swimming towards the shore: it's a lot farther away than you think, just as soon as you think you are getting close to it.

I switched strokes to see if that might help. I went from the breaststroke to the sidestroke until I ended up doing a frantic dog paddle. That's when this strange sensation came over me. It was a blend of absolute terror laced with a nice warm sleepy feeling. I had to make up my mind about which part of this feeling I would let win out. Then I remember something Mrs. Jamison had said about the dilemma I was now in. She said, if you were about to drown, the worst thing to do was to keep on swimming. It was better to relax and roll over on your back, or as she put it: "Don't fight it, let the water keep you afloat." I figured this was one of her "don'ts" that was worth doing.

I rolled over on my back and stayed that way for a long time until I felt my energy returning. I would float a little and then swim a little until I finally made it to shore. I staggered up to a nearby house and told the woman there what happened. She said I must have swum about thirteen kilometres, and that was pretty incredible for a nine-year-old. Then she called the Ontario Provincial Police, and one thing led to another, and I was sent back to the foster-kid depot.

~~~~~~~

I could have asked the swimming coach at school to help me swim Lake Ontario, but she had this irritating habit of blowing a whistle before she said anything. I hate whistles. I freeze up at the sound of them. When I explained this to her, she told me I couldn't go through life hating whistles. I told her I would go through life hating whatever I wanted to hate. That, and a few other things I said, got me expelled from swimming class.

My physics teacher, on the other hand, has never used a whistle. Her name is Mrs. Canyon. Some of the kids in the class call her "The Canyon." Because of her size, which is large, not so much vertically as horizontally. Rather than hiding her magnitude, however, she amplifies it by wearing dresses printed with huge glorious flowers that seem to sing out at you. "We are gigantic!"

I think she looks terrific – although she could do without those running shoes she wears. They make squishing noises with every step she takes, as if they're full of water.

Even though I've failed every test she's given me, she always writes things like "unusual angle" or "interesting approach" down on my papers instead of a big red "O."

I've never known anyone more excited about what she's doing than Mrs. Canyon. She is just crazy about teaching physics. Her eyes almost pop out of head when she's trying to drive into our heads that "The kinetic energy of the regular motion of electrons through a circuit must be supplied at the expense of some other form of energy."

Most of that stuff creates a fog in my brain, and I just want to go to sleep. But words like "energy" and "Motion" have made it to a clearing in my brain. Those two things are all a marathon swimmer needs.
~~~~~~~

Chapter Four

I knew the girl that Chester was kissing, which made the whole thing a million times worse. Her name is Lisa McIver. We got to know each other in art class while she was making a clay bird and I was making a clay ashtray.

Even though I had made it a life rule never to make friends with girls – you can't trust them – I was friends with her in a grudging sort of way. I guess I can't blame Chester for being attracted to her. She is very good-natured but in a really cloying way. I'm really bitchy, but in a really interesting, mysterious way. Plus, I'm unusually beautiful, which of course, scares guys off, and she's sort of ordinary-looking. No, none of that's true except for the bitchy part.

Like I said, I've never seen Chester up close, but Cupid's arrow can strike your heart from light-years away. It struck mine one day in history class. I was looking at Chester from across the crowded classroom. He was looking out the window, daydreaming. God only knows what he was daydreaming about, but I fell in love with the expression on his face.

The line of his mouth made my mouth feel wet with yearning. At that moment, I thought he was splendid. Now, of course, I think he's a bastard who belongs in hell.

I wonder what attracts us to someone else? Looks? Intelligence? Smell? I wonder what attracted Helen and Dan to each other? They have nothing in common. She's a fuck head. He's very kind. She's a librarian. He's a plumber. She's black. He's white.

Once, when they went out, I rifled through their bedroom to find something that would expose the true meaning of their relationship.

I did find something interesting in a weird place. It was their wedding picture, tucked into one of Dan's argyle socks. What seemed even weirder was it showed them both looking radiantly happy. Helen's smile looked real. They had their arms wrapped around each other and stood next to a neon-framed sign that read "Las Vegas Chapel of Love." I thought Helen would have had to be drugged and kidnapped before she would ever go to a place like Las Vegas. But what topped everything else was that Helen looked about eight months pregnant.

I started singing a version of an old Motown song: "Goin' to the chapel, cuz I *have* to get married..." and slipped the picture back into Dan's sock drawer.

` ` ` `

Every morning, like clockwork, I would hear Helen's prison matron's voice through the pillow I had crammed over my head. "Time to get up, Penny."

Even though I had an alarm clock, she would call me just before it went off and then leave the room with a quick sharp slam of the door. She just couldn't stand to let me have that five minutes of extra sleep.

I would hear Dan coughing in the bathroom: his regular throat-clearing ritual before his first cigarette. I would grope under the bed for mine, which I had bought with money I had stolen from Dan's wallet. I figured he wouldn't really mind.

The first cigarette of the day always tastes the best. Why is it that things that taste the best are always bad for you? It's like your taste buds couldn't give a shit about what your brain is telling them. It's that moth-to-a-flame thing again. I planned to quit cigarettes once I started my training.

Helen had unpacked my clothes. It was strange how she did that without saying anything to me about it. She had probably searched through my things for drugs. Except for nicotine and a few hits of pot, I haven't used anything else so far. But now my bedroom looks a little more like I'm living in it. I even dared to tape something up. It was a huge poster of Albert Einstein. Helen was very impressed. But I didn't put it there to impress her. I was hoping to impress Mrs. Canyon by telling her about it, except that I put it up after I had told her about it.

I would lie in bed sending smoke rings over to good old Mr. Einstein. I wondered if Mrs. Canyon knew the speed of smoke rings traveling across a bedroom.

She would probably say that it would depend on the initial energy they were sent off with. If I could figure that out, I could figure out how to send a rocket to the moon.

The morning after I had decided to swim Lake Ontario when I finally made it to the kitchen for breakfast, Helen and Dan were talking about summer vacation. Helen wanted to spend it throwing all the trash out of the backyard, which would have meant throwing out the grass because there was nothing else out there. Dan wanted to go camping.

"And get ripped apart by a rampaging bear?" Helen asked. She would always rampage right through any of Dan's ideas.

"Ain't no way a bear could get past you, Helen," Dan said with that same teasing smile he always used when he was talking to her.

"There is no way," Helen shot back. "*Not ain't.*"

"There is no fuckin' way a bear could get past you, Helen."

A big ball of laughter came shooting up my throat, but I held it back.

"D-A-A-A-A-N!" Helen shouted, stretching out his name to eight syllables. "How dare you use that word in front of a child!"

"Helen, she's sixteen years old, for Chrissake. I betcha she uses it all the time. Right?"

His question was directed at me.

"Only accidentally," I answered.

Dan laughed, but Helen put her sights back on me. "Well, you won't ever use it in this house."

I nodded. Fuck you, Helen.

Dan asked me if there was anything special I wanted to do for the summer. I told him I wanted to swim Lake Ontario. He spilled his coffee. Helen just stared at me with a pulsating ring of white around her irises.

"You wanna what?" Dan asked even though I knew he had heard me the first time.

"I want to swim Lake Ontario," I repeated.

It was strange what it sounded like when I actually said it out loud. It was like listening to another person say it.

Dan laughed, but Helen remained serious. It was the nicest thing she had done up until then. Then she had to ruin it all. "You should read *Swim to Glory*. It's the story of how Marilyn Bell swam Lake Ontario.

She started training when she was nine years old. She swam for hours and hours every day. You'll think twice about wanting to swim Lake Ontario after you've read that book."

Why would I want to read a book that would put me off swimming the Lake? The urge to tell her to fuck off was almost overwhelming, but I held it down. I wasn't ready to give up having my own room yet. Instead, with awesome politeness, I asked, "Is that book in the library?"

"Of course, it's in the library." She replied. I'll bring it home for you."

I wasn't allowed to say thank you, so I nodded eight times.

Dan got up to get more coffee and mumbled. "Ain't that something."

"Well, see you all later," I said, backing out of the kitchen. Once out in the hallway, however, I snuck back to listen.

"Mrs. Horshaw said to expect something," I heard Helen say over the violent rattle of dishes being placed in the sink.

"Oh, she's not serious," answered Dan. "You know how kids are."

"No, I don't know how kids are, and neither do you." There was a frailty in Helen's voice that I had never heard before. It made me feel uneasy about hating her so much like I felt just before I killed this big ugly bug that was trying to stroll across a room I was in once. But the feeling only lasted a nanosecond.

I heard Helen approaching the doorway, and I took off.

Outside that morning, it was sunny, but there was a sneaky cold breeze blowing about that took you by surprise. There must be whitecaps on the Lake now, but if I dove into it and went deeper and deeper, it would be very dark and still. Down there, the Lake would whisper its mystery to me.

I felt so cold. I pressed my arms to my chest. I had left my jacket in the kitchen. I didn't want to go back to get it. I didn't ever want to go back to the Normans, no matter how much I needed my own room. My bullshit shovel was getting too heavy to lift.

I had spent my whole life putting up with people who had to put up with me. I couldn't wait to be eighteen, and then I would be free. I wanted to keep on walking until my legs fell off, but when I reached the corner of the Normans' street, I saw the bus coming and decided to take it to school.

The usual people were on the bus. I sat down next to this old guy who dressed in a variety of plaids. I called him Mr. Tellme because he was a complete news junkie. He read newspapers while listening to a transistor radio tuned into an all-news station. I could understand his addiction. It was better hearing the news of the world than the news of your own life.

I looked over at the two women sitting across from me, whom I had named Dow and Jones. They were always dressed in Bay Street suits. They had just started another installment of what I called *The Saga of the Fucking Bitch.*

"All I said was that I needed an extra day to finish her report, and she went ballistic," said Dow.

"Don't let her get to you," said Jones.

"I'm trying not to, but the fucking bitch is driving me nuts. I mean, what does she think I do all day? I work my ass off, that's what I do, but according to her, that means nothing."

"Nothing you do is enough for her, but you just can't let her get to you."

I was in total agreement with Jones. That was exactly how you dealt with fucking bitches, two of who came immediately to mind, Helen and yours truly. I wonder why women turn into FBs. I know why I had. I had never been loved, but what was Helen's excuse? She was loved in her foster home. Dan loved her, for which he should be given the Nobel Peace Prize.

What more did she want? She must have wanted that baby she was carrying before they got married. It must have died, and she was still mourning for it. It would be wonderful to be mourned for.

I looked over at a couple I had named Eleanor and Rigby after the Beatles' song. They both had that single, never-been-married-in-their-late-forties look.

They got on at different stops, always managed to sit together, but always made out like they were totally oblivious of each other. They preferred their Stephen King novels, which they read in perfect synchronicity, turning their pages simultaneously.

I read a lot, so I know my way around words like "synchronicity." I know what a lot of words mean, but there are some I can't pronounce. The worst one is "aluminum." It comes out differently every time I say it. What does all this mean? Nothing, I suppose, but I keep on trying to say it. I whispered it out loud to myself on the bus. "A-loom-num-num." I thought about whispering it out loud again, but Dow gave me this look I'm sure she reserves for bag ladies.

The bus stopped to pick up a young woman I had named Eve, who was carrying a baby I had named Cain. Eve always looked weighed down with despair, but Cain looked like he could blow you away. He always had this hard little frown on his fat little face. I had tried coaxing a smile out of him, but it was like getting a rock to smile. That day, however, I gave him the meanest look I could muster.

It cracked him up. He gave me this drooling two-tooth smile. This made me want to stay on the bus when it stopped at my school, but I got off at the last moment.

I should never trust my last-moment decisions because the first people I saw were Lisa and Chester. To make matters worse, they were holding hands. I felt like I was two inches away from an ongoing train. I prayed to every God I had ever heard about to make them pass me by. My prayer was brutally ignored.

"Hi, Penny. Chester, this is Penny. Penny, this is Chester." Lisa said in that perky-pesky voice of hers.

Chester nodded in my direction like I was a telephone pole.

"Are you all ready for the exam?" Lisa asked.

I suddenly remembered I had a physics exam to write that morning. In fact, I had to write a whole pile of exams that week if I wanted to finish my year.

I must have been thinking about that for a while because Lisa said, "Earth to Penny. Earth to Penny."

Chester laughed. My skin went from goosebumps to feeling like it was on fire. I hoped he would soon be hit by a cement truck.

How could I have ever been attracted to him? It's because I had never seen him this close up before. He had a line of ripe pimples running along his jawbone, and his eyebrows met at the bridge of his nose. I walked off without saying anything, hoping I would look cryptically cool.

"What's with her?" asked Chester. He didn't even bother to wait until I couldn't hear him.

"She's got lots of problems," answered St. Lisa of Cloying.

I turned around to shout an obscenity but was intercepted by my untied sneaker lace, which I stepped on. Then I tripped and hit the ground like a landed mackerel. Oh, how much I wanted to be in the Lake at that moment, swimming through one foaming wave after another and then sinking into the Lake's comfort, leaving all this living behind me.

Lisa helped me up, brushed me off, and asked if I was all right. I told her I was fine but wished she would be burned at the stake like all good saints.

When I finally made it to my physics class seat, Mrs. Canyon, who was wearing a dress printed with a mob of giant daisies, greeted me with an exam paper. I read the first question: "The bow of a speedboat faces west, and the boat is driving westward fairly rapidly. In what direction does it first accelerate if the engine is started and the boat suddenly races forward?"

The question might as well have been written in Mandarin. An hour passed, and I was still wondering in what God-almighty direction that boat would move in. I drew a boat on my exam paper. Another hour passed. The boat had grown into an ocean liner. I had framed it with an intricate design of triangles and squares.

The bell finally rang. I stood up and dropped my paper on Mrs. Canyon's desk, picked it back up, and decided it would be safer in the wastebasket.

When I got home, Helen handed me *Swim to Glory*. She was really out to destroy my plan and me along with it. I promised her I would read it. When I reached the safety of my room, I tore the book up, page by page.

Chapter Five

The last day of exam week finally, mercifully, arrived. I had to swim the Lake more than ever now, and I had to ask Mrs. Canyon to coach me. I wasn't sure which of those two things would be more difficult. How could I ask her after putting her physics exam in the garbage? That must have impressed the hell out of her.

I found her in her office marking papers and asked her if I could retake the exam."

"Why?" she asked, "We both know you don't want to pass it."

Don't want to pass it? How could she say that? I wanted desperately to pass it. I just wasn't smart enough.

"However," she continued, "it's multiple-choice, so the odds are four to one that you might get the right answer, and I've never been one to stop anyone from trying to beat the odds." She handed me the exam and some paper and said, "I can only give you an hour. I want to be out of here by then."

I finished the exam, but I felt like I had finished gambling at a roulette table. When I handed her my paper, she said, "have a nice summer," without smiling. In fact, she looked angry because I had taken over two hours to finish the exam. I knew she wanted me gone, but I couldn't go. I felt that old feeling come back. The one I had felt around my parents. It was like being a mosquito. *Mosquito child's here. Get the fly swatter.*

"Now what?" she asked, becoming more piqued.

"Is it true that you knew Albert Einstein?" I asked only to give myself a little more time.

"*No*, that isn't true." Her voice was flat with sarcasm.

"What about Alexander Graham Bell?" I asked. My voice had gone up an octave.

"What about just getting out of here."

There was no way I could now ask her to be my coach.

But I had to ask her. And it had to be *now*. I was at the crossroads of either now or *never*. I felt I was about to jump off a cliff or that she was going to push me off. I had nothing to lose. I heard a squeak that sounded like a mouse. It was my voice. "Do you think you could help me swim the Lake?"

"What lake?" she asked, raising one eyebrow with mild interest.

"Lake Ontario."

"Can you swim?" She didn't look as shocked as I thought she would.

"Yes."

"Well, that's a start, isn't it. Now, what do you propose my role would be in your swimming the Lake?"

"It would be coach."

"But I'm a physics teacher, not Gus Ryder."

"Who's he?"

"He coached Marilyn Bell," she said, putting a series of "x's" beside the answers I had circled on my exam paper. "And you're no closer to being Marilyn Bell than I am to being Gus Ryder."

I thought that would be the end of it, but then she tore off a sheet from a notepad, scribbled something, and handed it to me. "This is my home number. Call me in two weeks if you still want to do it."

I took the slip and shot out the door like I had been fired from a cannon. I hadn't cried in years, but I did then. I ran bawling all the way down the hall – thank God it was empty- and crashed through the exit doors. Once outside, I stopped crying immediately. It was amazing how I could do that.

It was very hot. You could almost see the heat rising from the sidewalks, ready to boil you alive if you stood still for too long. The Lake would be smooth and calm now. I could be as fragile as a leaf floating on it, and it would treat me gently, lovingly.

I ended up at a park where I found a shady spot under a tree. I lay down and stared up at the dancing light between the tree's leaves.

Everything disappeared around me until there was nothing left but me and that dancing light. There were two other moments in my life when I felt that same sense of serenity: once when I saw an otter skiing on his back down a snowbank, and once when this lady spoke to me in Italian while she was watering her flowers.

After all, that serenity had worn out its welcome, I sat up and had a cigarette, which I vowed would be my last until I had swum Lake Ontario. I wasn't going to go home. It was about time I actually went down to the Lake. It was about time the Lake and I confronted each other. But instead of heading south, I went north to the McDonald's where Chester worked. This time I didn't care if I found him and Lisa making out on the counter. This time I was prepared. When I arrived, they were nowhere in sight. I felt disappointed in a way.

I ordered a Coke and fries and sat down at a table next to this Chinese guy reading a Chinese book. He looked about my age. Maybe a little older. It was hard to tell. There is something childlike about people's faces when they're reading a book. I wished that I had a book too. They give you something to do with your eyes when you're sitting alone in a restaurant.

No matter how hard I tried, I couldn't help staring at the Chinese guy reading his book. The writing in the book looked to me like a mumbo jumbo of crisscrossed lines.

English must look the same to someone who can't read English. I realized one thing: English has more circles in it than Chinese. I wondered how that came about. I wondered if anybody else wondered about that too.

The Chinese guy suddenly glanced sideways at me.

I pretended I had something in my eye.

I waited until he started reading again before I looked back down at his book. He immediately looked up again. This time he smiled.

"Is that book written in Mandarin?" I asked, hoping to sound very sophisticated.

He just nodded and kept on smiling. He could not understand English. I found this quite liberating.

"I hope I'm not interrupting your reading, but if I am, just tell me to fuck off," I said.

He kept on smiling. I continued with such a rush of words, it was like a dam bursting. "Last week, I had to write this physics exam, and the questions might as well have been written in Mandarin for all the sense I could make out of them, and now here I am sitting beside you, and you're actually reading Mandarin. Life is just a series of strange coincidences, isn't it?"

His constant smile made me go even crazier.

"How would you like to rob a bank with me?"

Just then, a Chinese woman with a young child hanging on to her skirt joined him. She was carrying a tray of drinks and hamburgers.

"Would you like to join us?" asked the Chinese guy in perfect English.

I was too embarrassed to say anything at first. Life at McDonald's was just one stunning humiliation after another. I shook my head, stood up, and said, "I was just kidding about robbing the bank."

"I know," he responded gently. "I hope you passed your physics exam."

I thanked him and tried to make as much of a nonchalant exit as I could.

There was nowhere else for me to go but back to the Normans'. They were both sitting in the kitchen. Helen said that I would have missed dinner if I had arrived one minute later because she didn't believe in keeping dinners warm for anyone. I told her I would not have any dinner just to teach myself a lesson. She told me she wasn't about to waste any food either, so I'd better eat what was on my plate.

Dan asked me how everything was going, and I told him I was thinking about applying for a job at McDonald's. He thought that was a terrific idea. But, of course, he didn't know it was a complete lie. I only wanted to say something that would ensure me a smooth departure to my bedroom, but as it turned out, I was headed for a crash landing.

It started when Helen asked me if I had read *Swim to Glory* yet. I told her I had ripped right through it. She asked me if it had changed my mind about swimming in the Lake.

I was going to lie about that too, but then Dan got up to get a beer. That's when everything I was struggling to hold back wouldn't listen to me anymore. I asked Dan if he would get me a beer too.

"No problem," he said as if I was asking for a cup of tea. "You want one too, Helen?"

"No, and don't you *dare* give her one either," Helen answered, still in shock over what I had requested.

I remained perfectly cool. I felt that I had won a small victory, even though I would be shortly giving up my own room.

"Oh, come on," said Dan. "I'll just give her one. After all, she's finished her exams. Probably aced every one of 'em too, didn't ya?"

I just nodded because I was sure my voice would give me away.

"Can I talk with you in the living room?" Helen demanded. She walked stiffly towards the door, and Dan obediently followed her out but rolled his eyes at me behind her back.

Why didn't she just say it in front of me? She knew I could overhear anything she said no matter where she went in the house. It was like living in an Ingmar Bergman movie.

"There is no way I'm going to allow you to give a sixteen-year-old girl a beer," Helen said, kicking off the fight.

"The French give their kids beer all the time," countered Dan.

"No, they give them wine."

"We don't have any wine."

"Even if we did, I wouldn't let her have any of that either. Besides, we're not French."

"I'm partly French on my mother's side."

"French-Canadian."

"So, that's still French. And they're more French than they are Canadian. Most of 'em want to separate from Canada."

I thought it was strange how their argument was veering off in all sorts of directions.

"What about you?" Helen asked. "Do you want to separate?"

"From Canada?"

"From me!"

"What the hell are you talkin' about?" Dad asked.

Helen came back into the kitchen. She looked like she wanted to kill someone. "I don't think this is working out," she said. "I think we would all be far happier if you were not living here."

"Fine," I said and added a shrug just to show her how much I couldn't care less about it.

"'That's all you can say?"

"Yeah, cuz I've got a headache." I stood up and headed towards the door.

"You do *not* have a headache!" she said, moving in to block my path.

How could she know whether I had a headache or not? I didn't have one at that moment, but I was starting to get one.

"And you're not going anywhere until I say what I have to say." She went through a complete metamorphosis right before me: from a librarian to a hissing tigress. I was waiting for her to sink her teething into my neck.

"You have been in my home for three months, and I have had to put up with your hateful hypocrisy, your deceit, your fucking *thank-you's!*" she continued, breaking her own commandment about the "F" word. "You think I don't see right through it! I know what you are! You're a lying little shit! You think you've had it hard! You think you've had a rough life! Well, you'll never know what I've had to put with!

You'll never know-"

"Oh, come on, Helen," Dan said, sauntering into the kitchen as if nothing was happening. "You never had it all that hard. You got a good education. You have a great job-"

At that point, Helen picked up Dan's dinner plate and threw it at him. He ducked, and it smashed against the fridge. She reached for another plate and threw that at him too. He ran from the room. I was too paralyzed with awe at Helen's rage to go anywhere. With one grand sweep of her arms, she cleared the kitchen table sending an avalanche of food, plates, and cutlery onto the floor.

She flung open cabinet doors, throwing out everything within arm's reach: plates, glasses, cups, saucers, bowls.

I stood still, but nothing hit me. I was miraculously safe in the eye of this china hurricane. By the time she had finished, she had broken everything in the room that was breakable except me.

It ended up with the two of us having this staring showdown. I stared right into those irises of hers, which were like black holes of rage, without flinching. She was the first one to lower her eyes. I felt like I could swim the Atlantic Ocean. She marched out of the kitchen, which now looked live in: a domestic battlefield. I marched to the front door, grabbing my jacket and Helen's purse on the way out.

Dan was sitting on the porch. I shoved Helen's purse under my jacket before he could see it.

"Where you going?" he asked as if nothing had happened.

"I dunno. Just out," I said, trying to sound like he was sounding.

"She'll be okay in a bit. Just give her time to cool off. It's my fault. I should never interrupt her when she gets into that thing of hers."

That "thing" of hers had just dropped a bomb on the kitchen, but it didn't seem to bother him. So, there was no way I was going to let it bother me. I just wanted to leave.

"Still wanna beer?" he said with a weak laugh.

"Nah, I think I'll just go for a walk."

"Kind of late to be out walking. Want me to come with you?"

"No, I'll be okay. I'm not going very far."

"I'll wait for ya,"

You do that, Dan, I thought to myself as I headed off. But you're going to be waiting forever.

When I was safely out of his sight. I ducked into some bushes to see what was in Helen's purse. I had hit the jackpot. There were about a hundred dollars in her wallet. More money than I had ever held in my hands at one time. I also found a pen and a notepad. I wrote a note saying, "I'll pay you back once I'm established." That sounded too much like I was starting a business. I ripped up that note and wrote another, "I'm sorry things didn't work out, but I'll pay you back as soon as I can." I was not sorry about anything, so that note was torn up too. I wrote a final note saying, "I'll pay you back," and put it under a rock by my foot.

I put the note pad and wallet back in Helen's purse and then peeked out of the bushes to check that no one was coming.

It was a good thing I did because I saw Dan approach. I ducked back into the bushes, made myself as small as I could, and prayed. My prayer was answered but with a hitch. Dan passed me, but just as he did, I felt something with multiple legs crawl down my back.

Once the coast was definitely clear, I took off down the street. I found a mailbox and crammed Helen's purse into it. There was enough identification in the purse for the post office to return it to her. My thieving always had a touch of integrity.

I felt bad about leaving Dan like that. He was the first nice guy I had ever known. I would have liked having him as a foster parent, but only if Helen wasn't living with him.

Chapter Six

I walked to the park where I had had my last cigarette. I would stay there for the night. No sense in wasting money on a room. I found a picnic table and crawled underneath it. I lay on my back and wondered what it would be like floating on the Lake at night.

I could see the stars through the cracks in the picnic table. I was in a cradle, and the Lake was rocking me to sleep. No, I was in a coffin. I bolted up and hit my head on the underside of the table.

You would think I would be quite at home sleeping in parks. I had done it on numerous occasions and had always kept those demons called Fear and Loneliness in their cages. But somehow, they had escaped. I started to cry. I was turning into the biggest crybaby on the entire continent of North America. I wished I had taken that Chinese guy up on his offer to join him and his family. I mean forever. I've seen enough families to know from the start how things would work out. I was absolutely positive life would have been serene with them. I would become Chinese. Maybe that was my problem. Regardless of what I looked like, maybe I was really Chinese.

While I scratched the first wave of mosquito bites that would plague me through that night, I wondered if asking for that beer had been a brave, reckless, or stupid thing to do. Probably all three. I had asked for something less controversial at Foster Home Number Three, or was it Number eight? Who knows? Who cares? Anyway, I had asked for an extra piece of toast. The result was straight out of Dickens.

"How much fuckin' toast you gonna eat?" asked the father, his mouth running with egg yolk. "We don't get *that* much money ta look after ya."

"Nobody in this house gets more than one toast with their breakfast," said the mother. "Just cuz yer a foster kid, ain't no way I'm treatin' ya different than my own kids." She backed this up by thumping her smallest kid on the back, which caused a geyser of CAP'N CRUNCH cereal to shoot out of his mouth and onto my face.

Maybe I'm the female version of Oliver Twist. I wouldn't mind at all. I would rather be a fictitious character than a real one.

My thoughts were interrupted by the sound of a car's horn. It was a steady honk-honk-honk. I counted each honk. Usually, the sound would have driven me crazy, but now it was comforting. The last honk was number thirty-four. The silence that followed made me feel even worse. I tried to feel better by imagining what all that honking was about. I imagined all sorts of things. They were all about love gone wrong. When does it ever go right?

There was someone else in the park now. From my picnic table bedroom, I could see a young guy tossing a Frisbee at an old black dog. The dog ignored the Frisbee.

His nose went up in the air. He had caught the scent of something more interesting. He trotted over to my table and crawled underneath it to join me. He wasn't the last bit puzzled to find me there. Dogs accept finding humans in all sorts of strange places. He licked my face a few times, then started barking – not angrily, he was just calling his owner to join him.

"Boris! Commere, Boris!" I heard the guy call.

Boris barked even louder. The guy came over to investigate. I had no choice but to crawl out from under the table. I tried to look as if I had been underneath it for just a short while, which was a pretty difficult thing to do.

"Sorry if he bothered you," said the guy. He had short spikey hair, and there was a score of tiny cuts across his chin. He hadn't quite mastered the art of shaving. He was painfully thin. His jogging pants were so loose that I feared they would fall down if he took in a deep breath.

"No, he's fine," I said. "I was looking for something I lost yesterday. I thought it might be under the table. But it doesn't look like it's there."

"What was it?"

"A ring. It belonged to my grandmother." I felt my mouth go dry. My heart started pounding in double time. I was walking on a tightrope across Niagara Falls. Lying can be dangerously exhilarating at times.

"Gee. That's too bad. I hope it wasn't too expensive."

"I don't know how much it was worth, but it was my grandmother's prized possession. She gave it to me on her deathbed." I had now reached the summit of Liar Mountain.

"Gee. That's too bad." He was beginning to sound like a broken record. He was probably high.

"I've been here all night looking for it."

"All night? Kind of hard to find a ring in the grass at night."

"I mean since dawn," I said too quickly. I caught a flicker of disbelief in his eyes. Liar Mountain began to tremble. "I know it sounds crazy, but I was just so upset about losing it, I don't know *when* I started looking, but I'm so tired now. I think I'll just go home. See ya." I backed away from him.

"Wanna lift?" he asked.

"No thanks." He was probably a serial killer. I turned and started running. But something made me stop and look back. I saw him on his knees, searching through the grass around the picnic table. That changed everything. He was back to being just a guy. Still a little weird, though. His weirdness made me feel bad about lying to him. I yelled back at him, "I didn't lose a ring!"

He couldn't have heard me because he kept on groping around in the grass.

I yelled again. "I lied about the whole thing!"

This time he looked up. He waved, and I waved back. I didn't know what the wave meant. Had he heard what I said and didn't care? Or had he not heard and was just waving goodbye? I left without looking back.

It would have been kind of interesting, though, if he did find a ring, and it really did belong to my grandmother, whoever she was. I never knew my grandparents. My parents never talked about them or showed me any pictures. I wondered if they were still alive. I wondered if I had ever passed them on the street. Mrs. Canyon could be my grandmother. She would be about the right age.

It was going to be very complicated calling her up in two weeks. I'd jump off that bridge when I got to it. I would be jumping off a lot of bridges before I got to swim the Lake.

I decided the best way to get through the rest of the day would be to go to the zoo. I went there once with some other set of foster parents. They had to announce every animal like I was an extraterrestrial. "Those are elephants!" they'd scream at me. "Those are lions!"

"Those are the furry, aquatic, fish-eating mammals," I said, pointing to the otters, hoping they would get the point. They just looked at me like I really was an alien.

What made things even worse were they had this thing about me calling them Mommy and Daddy. I refused. I never called my real parents that. They thought it was childish. Anyways, not calling these kiddie zoologists Mommy and Daddy was reason enough for them to send me back. They told me I was "desensitized beyond redemption." And that I was an "incorrigible" child. I looked up "incorrigible" in the dictionary. It means "incurably bad or depraved; not readily improved." I proved their point by saying, "Fuck you, Mommy and Daddy," just before leaving.

＼＼＼＼＼＼＼＼＼

I got on the subway and tried to settle down for the long ride to the end of the line, but I felt angrier and angrier thinking about all of my foster parents, especially that First-Class, El Supremo Fucking Bitch Helen. She was jealous of the relationship I had with Dan. By the time I had reached the end of the line, I had devised a brilliant plan to help him get rid of her. I went to the nearest phone and dialed their number. Dan answered, and I hung up. I waited for about an hour and dialed again. This time Helen answered. I put on my best French accent. "Allo, eez Dannie zere?"

"No, she said, "He's out at the moment. Can I take a message?"

"Who eez zis?"

"His wife."

"Zat bastard. He nef-fair told me he was mar-reed!"

"Who is this?"

"Zis? Zis is Colette!" I slammed the phone down. I was angry, as Colette would have been if she had really existed.

A rush of sweet vengeance lasted about five seconds. Then the biggest load of self-disgust settled down on my shoulders. I had stolen Helen's money and tried to break up her marriage. Not even Helen deserved that. I called again, but the line was busy.

I made a solemn promise to myself that after I had swum the Lake, I would work with the poor in the City of Joy to make up for what I had done.

Chapter Seven

I was sitting on a bench, waiting for the zoo bus, when a woman sat down beside me. She had a knapsack flung over one shoulder and held a bus schedule in one hand and the hand of a little boy in the other. The boy had a miniature version of her knapsack slung over his shoulder. She looked about thirty. He looked about five. Both had bubbly blond hair. They were obviously mother and son. The little boy was asking a different version of the same question over and over again.

"When's the bus gonna come?"

"In a while," answered his mother.

"When?"

"Pretty soon."

"Pretty soon?"

"Yeah."

"How long?"

"In about a minute."

"A minute?"

"Yeah."

It was incredible how she kept answering him without a trace of impatience. Her voice never stopped sounding gentle. I wondered how long that little boy would have lasted with my parents.

"Maybe two minutes," I said. The mother laughed. I laughed too.

"What're you laughing at, Mommy?"

"At what the lady said."

I had never been called a lady before. It made me feel elegant.

"What did she say?" he asked, eyeing me suspiciously.

"Nothing, Joey," the woman said with a playful tousle of his hair. "The bus is going to be here any minute."

Joey smoothed back his hair as if he didn't like anybody messing with it and continued his interrogation. "Is she going to the zoo too?"

"I don't know," answered the mother.

He wasn't about to ask me. It was his mother he trusted to have all the answers. I didn't blame him.

"Is she going to the zoo?" he persisted.

Yes, I am," I answered, but this little info addict was still not satisfied.

"Why is she going to the zoo, Mommy?"

"To see the animals, Joey." The woman looked up at me and smiled a smile I wished my mother had given me. I couldn't resist telling Joey that I had a brother named Joey too. He wasn't impressed, but his mother was.

"Oh, really?" she asked.

"Yeah, He's about the same age. I was going to bring him along with me, but he had to go to a birthday party."

The bus arrived, delaying lying binge for a few moments. I sat on the seat opposite them to continue it. I told her that my name was Colette, and she told me her name was Marilyn.

Then I told her the entire history of my fantasy family.

"My father was a heart surgeon, and my mother wrote a column for *The New York Times*. I was born in New York, just off Broadway, but we immigrated to Canada after the Republicans took over. My parents had Joey late in life, so they decided to stay at home to raise him because they both had to work when I was growing up. I've got a summer job with the local TV station, but because I work weekends, I have two days off during the week."

Marilyn listened attentively enough though Joey kept prodding her with his why's, where's and when's.

When we got to the zoo, I realized that I had talked non-stop to her. I was worried she might think I was a motor mouth who couldn't shut up. I tried to make up for it by offering to pay for her and Joey to get into the zoo. She refused.

I thought she was worried that I couldn't afford it, so I told her I earned a hundred bucks a day. That's when everything almost fell apart. Her smile evaporated. I got a little desperate because I was totally counting on spending the day with them. I gave her a small piece of the truth. "I had a little fight with my parents," I said.

"That's why I'm really here, and I just feel a little bit lonely about being by myself today. But if you want me to leave you alone, I will."

"Do your parents know you're here?" she asked. Her smile was creeping back again.

"Oh sure. They gave me the money to come."

"I see. Well, you're certainly welcome to join us if you like."

"You sure you don't mind?"

"No, not a bit."

"I can answer any question Joey has about any animal here. I'm studying to be a zoologist." I was back on the inside lying lane, and everything was running smoothly again.

By the time we were halfway through the zoo, we were all completely at home with one another. Joey turned into the little brother I wished really existed. He even trusted me to answer some of his questions. They were all about the zoo animals. One of them was quite profound: "Do they ever get to go home?"

I told him that this *was* their home and they were very happy living in the zoo. I wasn't sure that was true. I don't think Joey did either. I guess we both needed that lie.

When we stopped for lunch, I told Marilyn about my plan to swim Lake Ontario. It turned out her mother had named her Marilyn in honour of Marilyn Bell. This was an incredible coincidence. It made me laugh. Marilyn laughed too, but her laughter drifted into sadness. "I always felt I had disappointed my mother, she said. "I've never done anything as...*big* as what Marilyn Bell did."

"I think you are the biggest person I've ever met," I said.

"What do you mean?"

"I dunno." At that moment I couldn't think of anything. I just wanted to make her feel better. I did. She laughed again.

"When are you going to do it?" she asked.

"Do what?"

"Swim the Lake."

"In about two weeks, if everything works out." That's if a miracle happened.

"I'll be rooting for you all the way." She gave me a hug. I wasn't prepared for it. I usually hold my breath if I think someone's about to hug me. This was a breathing hug. It felt good.

By the time the end of the day rolled around, I wanted to stay with Marilyn and Joey for the rest of my life. I had already won over Joey. Marilyn had let me buy him a stuffed kangaroo, which was further stuffed with a baby kangaroo. It cost me thirty-five dollars – one-third of my stolen life savings – but it was worth it.

If I could have picked out my own foster parents, there would never have been any problem. I had already found two ideal ones: the Chinese guy and Marilyn.

When we were leaving the zoo, Joey made the first move for me. He asked if I would like to come to his house. It told him it was up to his mother. She told me that I could visit them any time I wanted to. I took a very bold step. I said I didn't want to just visit them. I wanted to *live* with them.

Marilyn didn't say anything for one long minute. She was too busy looking stunned and embarrassed. "I am very honoured that you would like to come live with us, but I'm afraid that's impossible. I'm sure your parents love you very much, and the best place for you to be is with them."

For once, I had told her the absolute truth, and she responded by stabbing me right through the heart. I had trusted her, and she had thrown that trust in the garbage. Maybe I was doomed forever to be treated that way.

On the bus ride home, I kept my big mouth shut. Marilyn tried to get me talking, but she wasn't ever going to hear another word from me. Joey kept asking, "What's the matter? What's the matter?" until I wanted to slug him.

When we got off the bus, Joey started crying. He refused to say goodbye to me. Marilyn had a look like she was about to reconsider everything. I was tempted to tell her the real story. That might have really won her over, but I couldn't bear it if she still said no.

She gave me her phone number and told me to call her up whenever I wanted to. I knew she didn't mean this. She was just trying to make herself feel better. She had no problem saying goodbye.

I walked away from them without saying goodbye back, hoping this would make her feel even a small tug of regret, but it didn't.

She yelled, "Good luck with your swim!" before I disappeared into the subway.

ßßß

It was rush hour, so the subway was crammed with people. I had thought about screaming. That would clear a seat for me. I had blisters on each heel, and my calves felt twisted into a tight knot from all that walking. Would I ever get into shape to swim the Lake? I'm sure the Lake was laughing at me now. *You could never swim me. You don't have the calves for it. You don't have the guts for it.*

The car finally cleared. I sat down, and I decided to stay in that seat until the subway stopped running.

I fell asleep and dreamed I was in the Lake. The water felt as cold as death.

The only light came from the beacon of a distant boat. I swam towards it. My arms felt like they were encased in concrete, and my calves were screaming with pain. I could see the shadowy figure of a person sitting in the boat, watching me. I heard a voice that sounded a lot like Marilyn's. "Keep on swimming," it said.

"No, I need to get into the boat," I answered, swallowing some water. It tasted like castor oil.

"You have to keep on swimming."

I choked on the slimy taste in my mouth. I swallowed more and more of it. My lungs filled up with this crap. I gave up and let myself sink. I was no longer cold and afraid. The water was now as comforting as a warm bowl of vegetable soup.

Nothing I dream about is strange to me, even after I wake up, but this dream was. I sunk right through Helen and Dan's living room. They were both sitting on the sofa smiling at me, not the least bit concerned.

As I sunk past them, they waved me a last *bon voyage*. As I sunk deeper into the watery darkness, a bunch of kangaroos circled me. They were wearing boxing gloves. One of them boxed me in the shoulder, first in a fun-loving way, but then it got rougher and rougher. "Wake up! Wake up!" it repeated. But why was it wearing a transit uniform? "It's the end of the line," it said. When I opened my eyes, its face dissolved into the face of the subway driver.

"Everything okay?" he asked me.

I got up and ran out of the subway and didn't stop until I was out on the street.

I felt so incredibly alone that I almost considered returning to the Normans. No, I would not do that. I just had to get used to being on my own. I had sixty dollars left, but what would I do when that ran out? I would get a job. I looked a lot older than I was. I would get a job at a TV station reading the news. But Mrs. Horshaw would see me, and that would be the end of that.

I would get a job at the McDonald's where Chester worked. At least I could be somewhat close to him there. Why was I thinking that? I didn't want to be close to him. I hated him with a hot, holy hate. I would get a job at another McDonald's, preferably in Timbuktu.

I knew of a hostel I could go to, but the staff would ask a lot of questions that I didn't want to answer. I would find a cheap room somewhere.

I found this hotel that looked appropriately economical. The lobby looked and smelled like the inside of an old shoe. A tall man leaned over the front desk like a vulture. His eyes were so watery they were completely colourless. I asked him how much the rooms were.

"That depends," he answered with a creepy grin.

I told him to keep his room from hell and walked out.

I was too tired to know where to go next. I ended up crouched in a telephone booth waiting for the sun to rise.

Chapter Eight

Once the sun was reasonably up, I called Marilyn. No sense in wasting being so close to a phone. I figured I owed her an apology for my behaviour. Having spent the night mulling it over, I decided it has been pretty ridiculous. Maybe she would invite me over. She did say I could visit any time I wanted to. I let the phone ring about twenty times, but there was no answer. Maybe she had given me the wrong number. I put her back on my hate list. I had no other choice but to head over to the McDonald's where Chester worked.

I was still in love. It was a rock-hard desperate love. When I arrived, he wasn't there. That was just fine. I needed to spruce myself up a bit. Quite a bit. Judging from my reflection in the washroom mirror, I looked like I needed a blood transfusion. There was also quite a variety of smells about me. So what. If I felt like shit, I might as well smell like it too. I went upstairs and ordered breakfast.

I had drunk about eight cups of coffee by the time Chester arrived. I was so high on caffeine, I felt I could walk through a wall. I went to his station. He remained expressionless, which was his normal expression. I asked for another cup of coffee.

"Small, medium, or large?"

"I don't' care."

His mouth twisted into a smirk. "Don't I know you? Yeah, you go to my school."

"Do you know my name?" I smirked back at him.

"I forgot it."

"Well, I know yours. It's Mr. Asshole." I turned around like I had on Zorro's cape and walked away. And then something incredible happened. *He followed me.* He moved in front of the door to block my exit.

"What's with you?" He didn't sound angry, just bewildered. I tried to answer, but my vocal cords had frozen over. Somebody from the counter yelled at him, "Hey Chester! You got customers here!"

He didn't look back at the counter. He just kept staring at me with one eyebrow slowing arching. It made me want to laugh, "I get off at three. Why don't you come back, and we'll talk."

All I could do was nod. I had turned into pablum. He went back to his counter, and I stumbled through the exit doors. My heart was pumping out more blood than my body could hold. It would burst through my skin. It was terrible. It was wonderful. I was so dizzy, but I wanted to whirl. I wanted to dance. I danced across the street and just missed being hit by a car. The driver yelled something, but I kept on dancing – right into Dan.

He was too surprised to say anything. So was I. We just stood rigidly in place as if a cosmic power had pushed a pause button. He spoke first. "Penny, where have you been? We've been worried sick about you."

I didn't answer. My mind was still off its hinges.

"My van's parked around the block," he said, taking my arm. "Come on. Let's go home."

I should have put up a fight, but he looked too frail to fight with. He didn't say anything else until we got to the van.

"Helen feels real bad about what happened. She thinks it's all her fault," he said, turning on the ignition. I wanted to tell him that it *was* her fault. She told me to leave, and there was only room for one maniac at the Normans. I remained silent.

"Please, Penny, give her another chance," he continued as we pulled away from the curb. "If you're worried about taking her purse, don't be. She just wants you back at home."

So that she can murder me, I thought. A wave of panic hit me. I was a prisoner in this moving van, driving closer and closer to ground zero. I needed to pee from all that coffee.

"You'll be free to go off on your own soon enough," he said. "But not now, Penny. You're way too young to do that now. You can swim the Lake if you wanna. You can swim the goddamn Atlantic Ocean, but give her another chance. Eh? Whadda ya say?" Suddenly the van swerved over to the curb and stopped. "This is crazy," he said. "I can't force you to come home. You'll just take off again, won 't you. So, if you wanna go, go." He didn't look at me. He just waited for me to leave. "Go on. I won't tell anyone I found you, but you can always call me up if you run into any trouble. I'll be there whenever you need me."

The "I'll be there whenever you need me" part won me over a little. It was just too hard to turn away from that, plus I needed to go to the bathroom. He pulled into a gas station and trusted me to return.

When I got back, we both sat there in silence for a long time. He was the first grown-up I could sit with and not feel I had to do anything to. The gas station attendant came over. Dan gave him a little salute and started the motor. We were back on the road again.

When we turned down our street, I could see Mrs. Horshaw's car parked in the Norman's drive. I felt immediately betrayed.

"We had to call her when you left, Penny," Dan said. "But don't worry, I'll straighten it all out."

I didn't give a shit about Mrs. Horshaw. I knew my way around her. But he should have told me about calling her. I refused to leave the van for a good ten minutes to teach him a lesson.

When I walked into the living room, Helen and Mrs. Horshaw were sitting on the couch. Both of them bolted up and glared at me like a firing squad.

"I know I should have called you first," Dan said before either of them could shoot. "But the important thing is I found her, and she's okay."

There was a momentary cease-fire. Then Helen screamed, "How dare you run off like that! You put us through hell!" Mrs. Horshaw patted Helen's arm to calm her down. Dan retreated into the kitchen. I stepped backwards to the front door. Mrs. Horshaw told me to "freeze." She had been a cop once. She read me the riot act about what happens to young girls who live on the streets. We're all supposed to end up as prostitutes or drug addicts, or both. I had never become either. I wanted to tell her this, but telling Mrs. Horshaw anything, once she shot got on a roll, was like stopping an avalanche.

Dan casually came back with a cup of coffee. Mrs. Horshaw's eyes narrowed on him. I knew what that meant. She didn't trust him. She didn't like nonchalance. She told him I would be better off in the girls' home where there would be more supervision, which basically meant being locked up at night. It's the end of the road for foster kids like me.

Dan pleaded with Mrs. Horshaw to give him another chance, and surprisingly Helen came to his defense. It should have been the other way around. Helen was the Class-A maniac. Why couldn't Mrs. Horshaw see that?

Maybe it was because Horshaw was late for her next case – she had a truckload of them – or maybe she just didn't care because I was allowed to stay with the Normans.

After she left, I was expecting Helen to nail me to the wall. Instead, she breezed off to her bedroom without saying a word. Dan went out to mow the front lawn.

I went to my room and watched the numbers clock by on my digital clock. I had two hours to go before I met Chester.

At 2:00 p.m., I headed to the bathroom for a thorough disinfection. I heard the muffled sounds of Helen crying when I passed by her bedroom door. I had never heard a grown-up cry before. It was kind of scary. She must have had another fight with Dan during my alarm-clock vigil. No, that was impossible. I would have heard them. Maybe I was too riveted to the clock to hear anything. I should have talked to her, but I was too afraid. I returned to my room and looked out the window. Dan wasn't out on the lawn, and his van wasn't parked in the driveway.

I went downstairs to the kitchen, but I couldn't find a shred of anything broken. A new set of china was arranged neatly in the cupboards.

I went upstairs again. The crying sound had changed into peaceful snoring. She must have had a bad dream. She was back to normal, at least what was normal for her, and I was back to wanting to be with Chester.

On the bus, I rehearsed how I was going to act with Chester. I would act angry; no, acting cool would be better; no, being nonchalant would be the best approach. I melded them together. I would be angry with cool, inscrutable nonchalance.

Once I reached the doors of McDonald's, my acting dissolved into confusion. I turned to leave. Then I turned around to go in. Then I turned to leave. Then I want in. Chester wasn't there.

He must be outside in the back, waiting to kiss me like he had kissed Lisa. He wasn't in the back either.

I asked a kid at the counter where Chester was. He told me Chester had left early. I told the kid not to tell Chester that I was asking for him. But I knew he would. So, I told him I was Chester's cousin from Detroit.

I was about to leave when Chester walked in. He was with Lisa.

"Chester told me what happened, and we'd both like to help you," Lisa said. Her eyes were filled to the brim with compassion. I hated pity. Especially coming from her. I told them that they could both go fuck their brains out.

***

Moments after my elegant exit from McDonald's, I realized I had nothing left. I deserved nothing. I was a liar and a thief. I was a selfish bitch. I was a nutball. I thought I could swim the Lake. It was just waiting to drown me. It had evil creatures living in its depths, ready to tear my flesh off.

***

Dan still wasn't there when I got home. I went up to my room. Helen's bedroom door was ajar. I couldn't hear her snoring. Maybe she had gone out. I went to my room, but the walls felt like they were closing in on me. I had to talk to someone. I thought about calling Mrs. Canyon, but what would I say to her? I returned to the doorway of Helen's room and whispered, "You okay?" There was no answer.

Something made me push the door open. I saw Helen lying asleep on the bed. She looked very peaceful. Too peaceful. I saw an empty pill bottle on the floor. My brain didn't want to add it all up. What if she was dead? No way I could go in there if she was dead. Let Dan find her. I would go back to my room and wait. She wanted to die, so let her be dead. Maybe she was almost dead. Maybe there was still time. I ran downstairs to the kitchen phone and dialed 911.

Chapter Nine

Helen was in the hospital for a week. Dan went to visit her. I didn't. I may have saved her life, but I couldn't stand living with her. I was hoping to enjoy a week of having Dan all to myself, but he wasn't home much. He was either working or at the hospital. All he said to me about what Helen had done was boiled down to one repeated statement: "She'll be up soon."

When Helen came home, she went straight to her room and stayed in it for two days. Dan told me not to worry. Worry? I was thrilled about not having to deal with her. He said the library had given her a month off to recuperate from her accident. How could anybody accidentally swallow a whole bottle of sleeping pills?"

On the morning of the third day, I went into the kitchen, and there she was, sitting at the table, sipping tea. She was swaddled in a ragged terry-cloth bathroom that had a major hole in one sleeve. Her elbow poked out of it. I had never seen her in this robe before or anything else with a hole in it. She was always strictly groomed. But what seemed even more amazing was her hair. She usually kept it plastered straight with gel so that it looked like a metal helmet. Now it was a joyous cloud of frizz. It reminded me of Mrs. Canyon's dresses.

What should I say? What was appropriate? I had a million questions about suicide. But "Would you like some more tea?" was all I could ask for the time being.

"Yes, please," she answered very softly and very politely. Maybe they had performed a lobotomy on her.

I heard the lawnmower startup. Dan was in the backyard cutting the grass, as usual.

I can't stand the sound of lawnmowers or any motorized cutting thing. But at that moment, it was welcome interruption on the heavy silence of the kitchen.

I plugged in the kettle, waited for a moment, and the big question popped out. "What was it like?"

She gave me this Mona Lisa smile. She wasn't about to share that secret.

"How come you did it?" I asked. This time I could see a little charge light up her eyes.

"You can't live without love, Penny," she said. Her voice took on its usual hard edge. "You just can't. You should know that. Nobody has ever loved you have they? I still have enough pills for both of us. What do you say we end all this shit right now?"

Things were getting even more deranged at the Normans' "Want some more tea?" I asked again. Helen laughed. It was the first time I had ever heard her laugh. It sounded canned.

Through the window, I could see Dan's head pass by in a Blue Jays cap. It was like parallel universes. He was in the Norman Rockwell one, and I was in the Salvador Dali one with Helen.

"Nothing gets to you, does it?" she asked. "And if that makes you happy, kiddo, you'll be the first that it ever did make happy. No, that's not right, but it's pretty close to that line from Dorothy Parker's poem. Have you ever read her?"

I had read everything Dorothy Parker had ever written. She was my Goddess of Literature. "No, I've never heard of her." I still didn't want to tell her the truth about anything I did.

"Neither has Dan," she said, "Of course, he's just barely heard of Shakespeare. He summed up his works by saying they were just a lot of beatin' around the bush. How could I have ever married him? How could I have ever loved him? Nigel will always have my heart. Now there was a man to love. He had so much passion. He was an artist, A great big motherfucking artist. We would have been a pretty glorious couple by now. I would have become a famous writer instead of a librarian. I would have had a whole life instead of this empty hole. Dan doesn't care. He's been cheating on me, you know. Not that I blame him. He must know I don't love him."

I suddenly remembered my Colette call. Now was the time to come clean, but that would have taken someone braver than me.

"He deserves so much better than what I have given him," she continued. He's a good man. It was his idea to become a foster parent. He thought it might help me get over losing Nigel's baby."

"Nigel's baby?" I asked.

"When I got pregnant, Nigel told me we had no right to take on the responsibility of raising a child if we were going to dedicate our lives to art. It would not be fair to the child or to ourselves. He wanted me to have an abortion. I couldn't go through with it. He left for Europe, and I stayed here. I met Dan when I was six months pregnant. My toilet overflowed one night, and in walked Dan The Plumber. Never in a million years would I have thought I would end up marrying a plumber. But I desperately needed someone. I felt so terribly alone. So, I married Dan. My son was born with a heart defect and only lived a few days."

We were both startled by the shrill whistle of the kettle. "I don't want any more tea," Helen whispered with a sigh. She got up and headed for the door. "And I don't want any more of my life."

Was she going to take more pills, or what? I ran outside to get Dan. He was leaning against the lawnmower handle, which was still running and looking up at the sky. He turned off the motor when he saw me. "Helen up yet?" he asked.

"She was up for a while. Now, she's gone back to bed. Maybe you should go in to see her."

"What's that matter with her "?

"Everything."

"Oh, shit." He took off his cap and walked wearily towards the house.

Chapter Ten

I stood on the edge of the Scarborough Bluffs, looking out at the Lake. I felt like a minnow staring into the eye of a blue whale. I had finally gotten up the guts to confront the Lake. It was one thing to imagine it in the comfort of my bedroom, but it was something else to confront it face to face. The Lake sure had a mighty big face. There was no way I could swim in. How had Marilyn Bell gotten up the nerve?

I had read *Swim to Glory*. I bought another copy of it when Helen was in the hospital, with the money I had stolen from her. I'll say one thing for Helen, she never did ask about the money. I guess she had too much else on her mind, like killing herself. I didn't want to think about that. Dan would take care of her.

After reading *Swim to Glory, I* realized that Marilyn Bell and I had nothing in common. Lucky her.

I would call Mrs. Canyon and call the whole thing off. I phoned from the nearest phone booth.

"Penny who?" she asked after I told her who I was.

"The one who was going to swim Lake Ontario."

"Oh, yeah, now I remember," she said. She gave me the directions to her house and hung up before I could say anything.

Chapter Eleven

Mrs. Canyon's house wasn't what I expected. It was supposed to be a great-dilapidated mess. Instead, I faced a neat cottage with an orderly bed of flowers and a trimmed hedge.

When she opened the door, five cats scampered out, and five scampered in.

"Are you allergic?" she asked.

"I don't think so," I said.

"We'll soon find out. Come on in."

The feline caravan followed us down a narrow hallway lined with photographs of assembled students. She must have been teaching for a long time. She paused at one picture and pointed to the face of a guy in a leather jacket. His hair was combed forward in a slick curl. "He works in the space program now."

Her kitchen was small, but it had so much stuff in it. There was a table that looked like it had been a door at one time. It was set with a computer, a printer, and a stack of *Omni* magazines, pads of graph paper, newspapers, paper, and more paper, and one plate with accompanying cutlery. A rack of her huge dresses was dripping dry along one wall, but there was still enough space for the fridge, stove sink, counters, and cupboards. How did she fit it all in?

"Don't ask where I got all these cats, she said, opening the fridge. I started with one, and the rest is history." She took out a bowl of this pasta concoction, motioned to me to sit at the table, and plunked the bowl down in front of me.

"Help yourself. I couldn't finish it all myself, which brings me to the subject of diet. Not mine, of course." She took out a Molson's from the fridge and yanked off the cap. "Swimmers need to consume a lot of carbohydrates. A carbohydrate is an energy-producing organic compound of carbon with oxygen and hydrogen. For example, starch, sugar, and glucose. Starch is found in bread, rice, and pasta. No wonder

Michelangelo had the energy to paint the Sistine Chapel – it was pasta that gave it to him. And look at the Chinese building the Great Wall – it was rice that did it"

At that point, I was convinced that swimming the Lake was just a matter of diet. As the hours passed, however, she went from the topic of carbohydrates to calories and on to specific heat capacity.

I guess she was more of a physics teacher than a swimming coach. Nevertheless, when I left her kitchen, my plan to swim the Lake was back in action. I bought sixteen packets of spaghetti with my leftover stolen money and headed back to the Normans'.

Everything had turned around. Helen was in the backyard mowing the lawn in her bathrobe. Normally, this would have been tantamount to her being naked outside. Dan was in the kitchen having tea. Life was crazily under control in Norman Land.

Dan asked why I had bought so much spaghetti. He smiled for the first time since Helen's accident when I told him it was for my diet to swim the Lake.

"You're still plannin' on doin' that?" he asked.

"Might as well."

"Yeah, might as well. I mean, there's nuthin' wrong with havin' a big plan. I had one when I was your age." He stopped there. I sensed he wanted me to ask what it was, but he needed to be coaxed. I was turning into the Normans' shrink.

"What was it?" I could no longer stand that look on his face.

"Oh, it was nuthin.'" I knew the "nuthin'" was a big "something."

He dumped his tea in the sink and took out a beer.

After a few long gulps, he waded into what he wanted to tell me. "I've never told anybody about it before. But if I tell you what it is, you've gotta promise not to laugh."

"I promise." Why is it when people make you promise not to laugh at something they're about to tell you, it's usually something you would not have laughed at anyway because it's usually profoundly sad, but then they usually laugh at it themselves, which means you end up having to laugh at it too so they won't feel so embarrassed?

"I never really wanted to be a plumber."

I figure that was it. "Well, there's nothing wrong with that."

"Just hang on. There's more. Just give me a sec to think about the right way of explainin' it." Down went another long gulp of beer. He belched and continued. "My dad was a plumber; so was his dad, so were my three older brothers. It was one of those family traditions. Rob's the oldest, Kenny's next, then Mike and then me. They and my dad all still live in Espanola. I'm the only one who moved to the city. I was born ten years after Mike. My mom said it was such a surprise to have me, she went into labour still thinkin' she wasn't pregnant. I guess me bein' such a surprise, and bein' her last baby, made me kind of special to her. She took me everywhere she went: grocery shopping, clothes shopping, shoe shopping, wedding showers, baby showers – all women things – but I had a great time.

"But the best place she took me was where she got her hair done – Beverly's Beauty Basement. Bev was my mom's best friend. My mom thought Bev was the smartest woman in the world 'cause Bev ran her own business, and she ran it right in her own home.

"I loved goin' there. The other customers use ta fuss over me, lettin' me drink as much pop and eat as much candy as I wanted to. I would fill up on that candy and listen to them laugh and talk. They'd talk about everything. They had a solution to everything. Bev used ta say, 'The prime minister should have a direct line to this basement, 'cause we know what's to be done, and he should *do it*.'"

"Those women didn't just go there to get their hair done. They came there for all that talk and laughter. The only time I ever heard my mom laugh; I mean right from the gut, was in that basement.

"As I got older, my dad started in on my mom about takin' me there. He thought it would turn me into a sissy, so my mom and me had to keep it a secret. To this day, I think my dad still thinks he put a stop to me going to Bev's. But I didn't stop goin'. As a matter of fact, I started workin' there.

"First, I just swept up the cut hair, then I started washin' hair, and then Bev started to teach me how to cut hair. Bev told me that hairdressing wasn't a job a man should be ashamed of. Some of the best hairdressers in the world were men. Like Vee-dal Sassoon. I soon worked my way up to givin' perms and doin' dye jobs. Soon enough I could pretty well call myself a hairdresser.

"So, to finally cut this long story short, my big plan at sixteen was to open my own beauty parlor." He laughed, and I had to laugh along too, but I wanted to cry.

"Mom died about two months after my sixteenth birthday," he continued. "And Bev followed suit about a year later. Both of 'em died from heart attacks, 'cause both of 'em smoked three packs of Philip Morris uncorked a day," he said, lighting up. "And I guess my big plan died with them."

"But have you ever thought about still doing it?" I asked.

"There's no way I could do it now. I make a great livin' as a plumber, more than I would ever make if I opened up a beauty salon. Besides, I just don't have the same feelin' about it. As you get older, your plans get smaller and a whole lot less interesting. You'll understand that soon enough," he said stubbing out his cigarette. "Now why don't we whip up a batch of spaghetti with all that pasta you bought"?

I wanted him to talk more about his plan, to make him feel better about it, to give him some advice. But what grown-up is going to take advice from a fucked-up sixteen-year-old, or even a normal one if there is such a thing?

He took out a bag of tomatoes from the fridge. I could tell by the way his shoulders were tensed that he was holding back a lot. He chopped those tomatoes a little too vehemently. I peeled some onions, which made me cry. Thank God for onions when you need them.

Chapter Twelve

I stayed up late that night, just lying in bed plugged into "A Day At The Races" by Queen. I listened to it over and over again, trying to figure out Helen and Dan. They had fucked up their lives, like mine was on its way to be fucked up. So what if I swam the Lake? Not that I ever could. But what if I did? What would that make me? I'd be famous, but for what? Swimming Lake Ontario. Big deal. All that would prove is that I could punish my body like Marilyn Bell had punished hers.

It was just a huge waste of energy for no purpose.

The Lake had a purpose just by being a lake. It wasn't trying to prove anything. It didn't need to swim me. It didn't need anyone or love anyone. It didn't' love me, and I didn't love it. I wanted to master it. But what for?

There would be no trace of myself after I left the Lake. It wasn't like creating something.

Michelangelo had created something: that big painting on the ceiling of the Sistine Chapel with Adam and God almost touching fingers.

I could never figure out that part of the painting. I mean, what was really going on there? If Adam was supposed to be given his soul after God touched his finger, then why did Adam look alive without a soul? He was alive enough to stretch out his finger. Why wasn't he just a big empty ball of something, like a cloud? Maybe God was trying to get Adam's attention, but Adam wasn't paying any attention, so God stuck out His almighty finger at him and yelled, "Hey you! Listen up!"

When I was thinking about this, Freddie Mercury was just reaching that part of the song where he starts chanting about finding someone to love. It made me bolt upright. That's what God was saying to Adam: "Hey you! Find me somebody to love!"

But Adam pointed his finger right back at God and said, "First, You find me somebody!"

My mouth tasted slimy as if I had taken a swig of castor oil. It made me gag. I ran on tiptoes down the hall and just made it to the toilet bowl on time. I vomited up two platefuls of pasta.

The next morning, Helen was at the stove making pancakes, whopping big ones that filled the whole pan. She had on an I-mean-business suit, and her hair was back in that gelled helmet. She gave me her customary blank smile and said, "Dan told me you needed to eat a lot of carbohydrates for your swim."

This was even more of an unexpected turnaround. Why was she now on the pro side of me swimming the Lake? Well, it didn't matter what side she was on because I had changed my mind again. I wasn't going to swim anything. And I wasn't in the mood to say anything either.

"Sorry, but I'm not hungry."

"If it's because of what I told you yesterday, I want you to know that just because my life is over, it doesn't mean yours has to be. I was wrong to be so negative about your plan to swim Lake Ontario. I'm going to help you reach that goal," she said, lifting a pancake the size of a Conestoga wagon wheel. She flopped it onto a plate and slammed the plate down in front of me.

"I'm trying to take the first step away from the abyss, and if I'm willing to do that, you can at least eat my *pancakes.*"

Oh, Dear God on the ceiling of the Sistine Chapel, will Helen ever get out of the deep end?

I cut into the pancake. A blob of white guck seeped from it. No wonder; it would take a laser beam to cook a pancake this thick. I felt sick looking at this oozing mass, never mind taking a bite of it. I thought of those starving children I'd been told to think about whenever I turned down food – all those swollen-bellied babies on TV with flies on their faces. And here I was with my puny little problems when they were in more pain than I would ever experience. I scooped up a blob of pancake, opened my mouth, shoved it in, and swallowed hard.

"I'm also going to check into some swimming clubs and see if I can find a good coach." She added, pouring out another pancake from hell into the frying pan.

"But I already have one."

"Who?"

"Mrs. Canyon."

"What club is she with?"

"She isn't with any club. She's my physics teacher."

"And she's a swimming coach too?"

"Not really."

"What do you mean 'Not really? Either she's a swimming coach, or she's not. Which one is it? "

"She's not a swimming coach, but she's the swimming coach that I want."

"Why?"

"I like her."

"Well, that's all very nice, but I'm sure I can find you a swimming coach you'd like. Leave it to me. I'll find you a great coach."

Dan entered in time before things got any worse. He looked hungover. Mercifully, Helen aimed her sights on him, "Have a seat, honey," she said. "I'm making pancakes."

That word "honey" was slipped so casually into her sentence. It amazed me. I had never heard her call him anything except Dan and always like he had dropped something on her foot.

"Well, thank you, but I just need a coffee...dear." The "dear" part was hesitant, as if he didn't want to say it but felt compelled to match her "honey."

"No, that's no way to start your day," Helen replied, handing him one of her monster pancakes. "Besides, we have a marathon swimmer at our table. Let's try to set a good example for her."

He looked down at the pancake, then at me. By his expression, I knew I had a fellow hostage. We were both trapped in Helen's be-nice-to-me-or-I'll-kill-myself cage. I didn't look when he cut into his pancake. I knew what lay ahead of him. We were both spared that ordeal.

"Well, I'm afraid I'm running late," Helen announced, walking at a brisk march out of the kitchen. "You should never keep your shrink waiting."

Helen was seeing a shrink? Maybe that would help. But more importantly, she was gone.

Dan and I got up in unison and slid the mess on our plates into the garbage.

"She'll settle down in a day or so," he said. "Every time she has one of her accidents, she always follows the same pattern. She gets really down, then really up, but then she evens out eventually."

"How many accidents has she had?"

"Oh, I dunno, I lost count."

"Lost count?"

He shrugged as if Helen's suicide attempt was just a regular slice of life.

"But the last one was less complicated. She usually...... "He was interrupted by the ring of the front doorbell. He went to answer it, and I pulled out the garbage bag. I was going to put it in the neighbor's garbage can. No telling what Helen might do if she discovered what was inside it. I was closing the bag up with a twist tie when Dan returned.

"There's a girl here to see you," he said, taking the garbage. "I'll hide this."

"But I don't know any girls."

"She's waitin' in the living room. See you later. I gotta get to work." He was out the back door just as I heard a timorous voice call from behind me.

"Hi, Penny."

Lisa. What a way to round out a perfectly fucking morning.

She looked like a mouse facing a cat. She blurted out the following without taking a breath. "I know this is a surprise. I was going to call you except I couldn't find your phone number, but Chester and I followed you home that time you left us at McDonald's, so I knew where you lived, but when we followed you home that time we weren't sure if it was a good idea to talk to you just then, because Chester was with me, and him being a guy and all, I thought that you might feel better just talking to a girl, you know, so after a while, I thought and thought about it like for a week, and decided I would just do it alone, so here I am, and I just wanted to know if everything was okay with you."

What in the hell was I supposed to say to that? It was just too complicated.

"It's okay," I said.

"Okay?"

"Yeah."

"Are you sure?"

"Yeah."

"I also wanted to know why you were so angry with us."

"I wasn't angry." When would she take the hint to get lost?

"You used the "F" word."

She couldn't even say, "fuck". What a mouse she was. What a nerdy, dorky, fucking mouse.

"I just got my period that day."

"Oh, I see. I understand."

She looked so little and nervous. It was really pathetic. What did Chester see in her? He could dominate her. That's what it was. Well, he would never dominate me.

She took in a deep breath to calm herself, then started winding up again. "I felt crummy too when I first got mine...I mean when I get mine. I guess you think it's really strange me coming over like this, but I've been reading this great book about confronting things – you know what you're afraid of. And I was afraid to come over here and...well, actually I was afraid of you. I really didn't know why that was until it dawned on me why it was. It was because you were so angry, and that is what I'm really afraid of. I'm afraid of people's anger, and I shouldn't be because I read in this book people get angry, mainly because they are afraid of *you*. I mean, you're afraid of me. Which was really quite astounding to me. And I just wanted you to know that you shouldn't be afraid of me, and I was worried that you were."

"I'm not." I couldn't believe this. She was crazier than me.

"I thought you were. And Chester was worried about you too."

"He was!" I slipped. That was supposed to sound more like a casual question than an exclamation.

"Yeah. Anyway, he and I have broken up because...well, there are a lot of reasons, but one of them is that I don't like the way he...Well, let's just say we've broken up."

She finally said something I wanted to hear.

It didn't matter. The way to Chester was clear again. It was so hard not to smile – not to cheer! – but I had to remain poker-faced.

"Have you got any plans for the summer?"

"Yeah," I said as flatly as I could. I wanted her gone more than ever.

"I mean, like right now." She was not the least bit affected by my tone. "Maybe you would like to go to a movie or something."

"I can't. I'm in this swimming program."

"Swimming?"

"Yeah."

"You mean learning how to swim?"

"No, I *can* swim, but this is for long-distance swimming."

"Really? My brother swam right across the lake at our cottage once. It was eight kilometres."

"Well, I'm planning on swimming Lake Ontario this summer." Now, why did I have and say that? I wanted to get rid of her, not impress her. But I was compelled to tell her because she didn't think I had anything to boast about.

"Oh, my God! *Really?* She screamed. "That's incredible! That's wonderful!"

Her enthusiasm threw me off balance. Her reaction was more encouraging than anyone else's, but then she was a nutbar.

"Wait till I tell my brother," she said. "I'm sure he'd' love to meet you. When would you like to come over and meet him?"

"Well, I'm gonna be busy with training and everything."

"How about at night? You don't train at night, do you? "

"Yes, Night and day."

"But you could just drop over for a few minutes. Why not tonight? He's usually home around seven. I mean, if I tell him you're coming, he'll *definitely* be there. Okay?"

I should have said no, but I knew only a yes would get her to leave. She took out a pink notebook that had a handwritten title, "Things to Do Today." It was framed with her own artwork: a vine of daisies.

How sweet. It made me want to puke. Plus, daisies don't grow on vines. She wrote down her phone number and directions to her house, in excruciating detail, tore off each hole of the paper from its coiled binding with painstaking care, folded it three times, and handed it to me.

After she left, I threw it in the garbage.

Chapter Thirteen

I had four hours to kill before my training session with Mrs. Canyon. I killed them by walking to her house instead of taking the bus.

If only I could be as great a swimmer as I am a walker. Once I walked forty-eight kilometres for charity. That didn't make much sense to me, though. I could've just gone up to some poor person and suggested if they walked forty-eight, I'd raise them a buck a kilometre. But then, if I were that poor person, I'd probably tell me to go fuck myself.

I think about fate when I'm walking. Every time I pass a stranger on the street, I wonder why we are passing each other at that exact moment. I mean the stranger's born and I'm born, and we live our lives – maybe in separate cities, maybe in separate countries – and we have all these things happen to us: great things, awful things. Then one day, for just one moment in all the time we're alive, for just one blink of an eye, was pass each other. What makes that happen?

I picture fate as a woman sitting at a card table in the aisle of a warehouse that's the size of infinity. She's wearing a black suit and a wide-brimmed white hat that's tilted down so that all you can see is her mouth, which is painted blood red and always set with rigid disinterest. On either side of her are metal shelves stacked with card decks.

Each deck represents a person. She picks out a deck and randomly deals out the cards. Every card means something, and whatever comes up is what comes up for that particular person. It's all chance. It doesn't matter if you're good or bad. Fate doesn't give a shit. You're just a deck of cards to her. Or maybe there's more to it.

All of this made me think about that guy I met in the park with his dog. I suppose I could go there again. I'd probably run into him, but there was no way I wanted to go through that grandmother's ring thing.

I counted the number of people I passed on my way to Mrs. Canyon's. By the time I had reached her house, the number was up to a hundred and six. I wondered how many of them I would ever pass again.

Chapter Fourteen

"What do your folks think about you swimming the lake?" asked Mrs. Canyon as she stood at her kitchen counter preparing an army of sandwiches. I was sitting at the table. Four of her cats were sitting on top of it. Eight unblinking cats' eyes were trained on me like an interrogation squad.

"Oh, they think it's great," I said, not looking at the cats.

"Really?"

It was hard to tell what that "really" meant. It fell somewhere between belief and disbelief.

"Do you have any brothers and sisters?"

"I did have one, but he died a few weeks after birth because of a heart defect." This was almost true. I mean, if Helen and Dan were my foster parents, then Helen's dead baby was my brother in a foster kind of way.

"How's your heart?" asked Mrs. Canyon, biting off a hunk of cheese.

I wanted to say that my heart was in hiding forever, but what came out was "okay."

"That's what killed my husband. One minute he was playing *I Can't Get Started* on the piano, and the next minute his heart stopped. After he was buried, I got rid of the piano. I hate the sound. Do you know how sound travels? It travels in waves, which are produced by vibrating objects...."

She was off again. I revved up the nerve to stop her. "Mrs. Cannon, I think sound is really interesting but-"

"But you're not interested in it."

"Sure, I am," I answered, trying to sound convincing.

"What is it that you find interesting about it?" she asked handed me a four-story sandwich.

"Lots of things."

"Name one."

"The speed it travels at. That's pretty interesting."

"How fast does sound travel?"

"Very fast."

She laughed a big booming laugh. The cats leapt from the table in four different directions.

"How fast do you think you can swim?"

"I dunno. I never timed myself, but I know how fast Marilyn Bell swam Lake Ontario.

She swam fifty-one kilometres...actually, it was fifty-six kilometres because the current dragged her off course.

She swam fifty-six kilometres in twenty hours and fifty-seven minutes. So, I guess she swam about two and a half kilometres per hour."

Mrs. Canyon was overwhelmed by this outburst of data, mainly because it came from me. I felt just as astounded. Normally I don't remember facts, but I remember those from reading *Swim to Glory*. And usually, I have to write down mathematical calculations, even to add ten plus two. Otherwise, the whole exercise just doesn't stay put in my brain. This time I had done one in my head and even converted it into metric. It was very strange.

"Well, now we're getting somewhere, aren't we?"

"Yes, I said, even though I wasn't sure exactly *where* we were getting *to*. But I had impressed her, and that was all that mattered.

"I think we're ready to get into force and motion. Let's start with motion. The study of why things move is called *dynamics*. You see that cat over there?" she said, pointing to a cat with battle-frayed ears. "I named him *Dynamo* because, unlike most cats, he rarely sleeps. He's always on the go. A force makes him go. One of the seven forces that makes everything go. There's gravitational force, tensile force, magnet force, electric force, elastic force, explosive force, and muscle force. Which one of those forces makes Dynamo go?"

My brain had probably blown a fuse. "I dunno," I said with a hopeless sigh.

"Sure, you do. It's what makes all of us creatures go: heart."

"Heart?"

"And what is a heart made of?"

"Well, blood and stuff."

"What other stuff? Concrete? Flour? *Muscle?*"

"Muscle."

"Brava!" she exclaimed, clapping her hands.

Even though she had fed me the answer, even though a five-year-old could have figured it out, and even though it wasn't the answer to anything big. I felt like it was. I felt exhilarated. My own heart muscles were beating up a storm.

It might take a long time before we actually got onto the subject of me swimming Lake Ontario, but it was now firmly embedded in my mind that Mrs. Canyon could get me to do it. I let her go on about force and motion for the rest of the afternoon without interrupting.

Chapter Fifteen

A new me swung through the doors of McDonald's. I could swim Lake Ontario, and I could win Chester's heart – now that Lisa was out of it. Chester and I would get married after I had swum the Lake. He would not be able to resist my fame. We would honeymoon in a Viking boat festooned with daises. The Lake would rock us when we went all the way. All the way? A kiss would be enough. Just once to feel his mouth on mine warm and moving. We would create an incredible universe where our love would conquer everything. I would be home at last.

Chester was at the counter when I walked in. Seeing him for real made my dream somewhat less romantic. Maybe I wasn't really in love with him. Maybe I was just in lust with him. Maybe that's why I had a hard time looking him straight in the eye. I went to the washroom without him seeing me.

I thought about masturbating on the can, but McDonald's washroom wasn't quite the place for it. To tell you the truth, I've never masturbated before. Every time I've tried, I've felt like I'm invading myself. I should do it. How else do you deal with this feeling?

Once someone had lustful feelings about me. It happened when I was fourteen. His name was Alistair, which I thought was pretty sophisticated. He was twenty-one. He lived with his parents, who fostered me for a while. He was studying to become a doctor. He took me to baseball games and movies. None of the movies were in English, and they all portrayed life a lot differently than what I was used to seeing. All their endings weren't happy.

Alistair came on to me during one of those movies. He put his hand on my upper thigh. It startled me, but then I pretended it wasn't there, which was as easy as pretending I was John A. Macdonald.

I let his hand stay on my thigh without doing anything about it, which I guess he took as a sign that I was turned on. And I was kind of turned on because he was really cute, and I really liked being with him. But at the same time, I was scared because it had turned our relationship into a whole different thing, and I wasn't sure if I was ready for that. Accidentally, maybe on purpose, I spilled my drink on his hand and on my pants. I walked through the lobby to the washroom, convinced that anyone who saw it would think it was semen.

Later that night, Alistair tried a more direct approach. His urgent whisper woke me up: "Penny...Penny...*Penny!*" He was standing next to my bed in his underwear. His kid sister was asleep in another bed two metres away. He told me he couldn't sleep. The pressure at school was driving him crazy. He didn't think he would ever become a doctor, and his parents would disinherit him if he didn't. He started to cry, and the next thing I knew, he was in bed with me, holding me so tight that I could hardly breathe. The turned-on feeling switched to a completely turned-off one. I struggled, but he was very strong.

The family dog intervened. He must have been bred to go berserk if he sensed someone was trying to have sex because he started barking outside the bedroom door, waking up Alistair's sister and his parents. The father came into the room just as his son was jumping out of my bed. That was the end of my stay with them.

So now it was my turn to have lustful feelings. At least Chester was my own age. Then I had to ruin that feeling by thinking about Lisa. Anyone who would just jump into someone's house, stumbling all over themselves to make friends was really desperate. She had made a pathetic fool of herself. Just like I had done with Chester. But I would not do that again. I was in complete control of myself.

Chester was at his command post when I returned. I gave him this look like I was surprised to find him there, which was incredibly dumb because we both knew he worked there. He gave me this slow smile, and I felt all shaky inside.

I ordered from the guy next to him in a voice low and sultry. The guy made me repeat my order because he couldn't hear me. I carried my shaking tray of Coke and fries over to a table and sat down.

Chester came over and wiped the table next to me, which was already spotlessly clean. He was the only guy I knew who could look cool in a McDonald's uniform.

"How's it going?" he asked.

"Fine," I said, then checked my watch like I led a busy, busy life.

"Haven't seen you around for a while."

"Haven't been around."

"Watcha been doin'?""

"Nothing much."

"Oh Yeah? Lisa told me you're goin' to swim Lake Ontario."

"She did?" I thought they had broken up. What was going on?

"How come?"

"How come what?"

"How come you're goin' to swim Lake Ontario?"

"Because...because...because..." Putting a lid on that word was hopeless. It kept coming out.

"Because why?"

"Because that's just the way things turned out." What the hell did that mean? Chester looked at me as if he was asking himself the same question. "And I've been doing a lot of marathon swimming, sort of working my way up to it."

"Oh yeah?"

"Yeah."

"Where?"

"Lake Simcoe."

"You swam Lake Simcoe?"

"Sixteen kilometres of it."

"Sixteen kilometres?"

"Yeah."

"You wanna do something?"

"Pardon?"

"You know, you wanna go out somewhere?"

"Well, I dunno, I guess so."

"How 'bout tonight?"

"I guess tonight would be okay."

"Meet me here at seven. That's when I get off." He walked off, whipping the back of a chair with his washcloth.

I sailed out of McDonald's. How glorious, how magnificent, how wonderful it was to be alive. Thank you, God, on the ceiling of the Sistine Chapel.

I sang a corny love song as I walked home, not caring who heard me.

Chapter Sixteen

Helen was in the dining room when I got home. I didn't want her to ruin my delirious state, but something else in the room made me do a double-take. She was transfixed by a crystal bowl that seemed to be floating in place, as whimsically as a soap bubble, over the dining-room table.

"Nigel gave it to me." She didn't turn around, but she knew I was there. "He made it."

"What's for dinner?" Dan asked in a normal voice, but it sounded like a cannon blast. He was standing in the archway of the dining room, wearing his plumbing overalls.

Helen and I both reacted with a start, terrified the sound would shatter the bowl. The illusion was broken. The bowl rested still, dead centre, on the table. Helen left without answering him. Dan gave a what-did-I-do-now look. I shrugged. I was determined to remain as neutral as Switzerland between these two warring parties, but I ended up following Helen into the kitchen.

She pulled a sheet of paper from her purse and handed it to me. "Here's a list of some great coaches I've found for you. Any one of them would be___ "

"But I told you, I have a coach."

"What?" She looked like it was the first time she had heard it.

"I already have a coach," I repeated. "Her name is Mrs. Canyon. She's my physics teacher."

"What does physics have to do with swimming"?

By her tone, I knew another explosion was about to go off. "Well, according to Mrs. Canyon, it has a lot to do with it."

"Like what?"

"Like energy and motion. You know, things like that."

"Well, *everything* has to do with that." She suddenly went limp and collapsed into a chair.

I remained cautious. The bomb might still be ticking. "Would you like me to help you with dinner?"

"No, I don't feel like cooking."

Dan came in like he was entering a minefield. "Why don't I take us all out for dinner and a movie?"

Helen actually smiled at him. Now things were going to get really tricky. Going out with them would probably be the right thing to do, but it would mean giving up my date with Chester. "I can't go with you," I said, "I have a...." I wasn't sure I wanted them to know about Chester.

"A date?" Dan asked.

"No," I said but blushed.

Where are you going?" Helen asked. I knew she had caught a scent of something.

"I dunno."

"It doesn't matter where you go when you're in love, does it?"

How had she figured that out?

"Then I guess it's just you and me, d-d-dear," said Dan.

"I'm not hungry," Helen replied, crushing her list into a tight ball. She tossed the ball at Dan. It bounced off his head and landed neatly in a mug on the table. It's one of those things that happen accidentally that would otherwise take years to master.

"Good shot," said Dan.

"I'm a terrific shot." It sounded more like a warning than a statement. Her smile had vanished. "Penny has more important things to do than be with us, don't you, dear."

That's a question grown-ups ask when they want to corner you. I've learned to remain silent in the corner.

"Never mind. I don't care. I didn't expect anything more from her." She left, adding a limp to her walk, just to heap more guilt onto me.

Well, let her try to ruin my one chance with Chester. She would never succeed. I would rot in hell first.

None of this affected Dan. "So, when's he comin' to pick you up?"

"I'm meeting him."

"You're meetin' him? He's in a wheelchair or somethin'?"

"No, I told him I'd meet him."

"Well, guess there's nothing wrong with that. What's his name?"

"Harry."

"Harry."

"I have to get ready now," I said, hurrying out of the kitchen. I didn't want to answer any more of his questions.

****

It took me over an hour to decide what to wear. I started out with the dress. My only dress. My legs didn't feel comfortable in it. They weren't used to being exposed. I put my jeans back on and pulled on a tight sweater, which brought me to the big problem about my boobs. They weren't big, but they were big enough to be noticed. Still, I wasn't sure I wanted Chester to notice them or for him to think that I wanted him to notice them. I put on a vest Helen gave me over the sweater so that my boobs would be noticed indirectly.

Trying to be sexually attractive is very complicated. At least for me, it is.

Then came the question about makeup. Should I wear more or less or none? If I wore more, he'd think I was trying to make a big production out of this because I was desperate. Desperate is the last thing you want to look if you're trying to look sexy, which I didn't want to look like. Or maybe I did.

If I wore less makeup, then he would think I was trying to look as wholesome as Lisa, who was the last person I wanted to remind him of. But if I don't wear mascara, I don't have any eyelashes at all. And without blush and lipstick, I look dead.

I wondered what Chester was doing to get ready. Probably nothing. Why do girls have to go through all this shit and guys don't? Never mind burning our bras – why don't we burn all our makeup? Girls wear makeup because most of them don't want to look like shit next to girls who do. So, if we all stopped wearing makeup, that would eliminate the entire problem. Right?

I was asking myself this question when Dan told me I was wanted on the phone. It couldn't be Chester because he didn't have my number. It had to be Lisa reminding me to come over. My guilt faucet was turned down again, but when I picked up the receiver, it wasn't Lisa's voice I heard.

"Bring your bathing suit tomorrow," Mrs. Canyon said. "It's about time you got in the water. Be here by five.""

"Five in the afternoon?" I asked hopefully.

"Five in the morning. That's the only time they'll let me use the pool."

"But I have a___" There was a click, and then the line went dead.

If I had to be at Canyon's house by five o'clock, that would mean I should be up by four, which meant I should be in bed by eight. No way. Besides, this whole lake-swimming thing was to get over Chester. But now that we were dating, or about to date, it had lost its *raison d'etre* (I think that means what I mean). I wanted to call her back and tell her, but that would make me feel even guiltier because of all the time and energy she had spent on me. How much guilt was I expected to carry around? It made me furious.

I went upstairs, put on a lot more makeup (even false eyelashes), took off my vest, and snuck out the back door.

When I got to McDonald's, Chester wasn't there, of course. So, of course, I would *not* be in love with him. He was a complete jerk. And so was I. I came up with ridiculous plans and put myself in ridiculous situations, like standing in McDonald's looking like a hooker. Both he and I should rot in hell together ... at least we'd be together.

With his usual timing, Chester showed up just as I was about to leave. He was an hour late. When he saw me, he gestured like he was reining in a horse.

"What happened to you?"

"What do you mean?" I asked and one of my false eyelashes sprung loose.

"I'm not taking you anywhere looking like that."

Like Miss Backboneless, I told him I'd be back in a minute and went into the washroom and washed off most of the makeup. When I returned, he was talking to some guys. I stood there waiting, but he kept on talking. Finally, he noticed me. "That's better," he said. I smiled like a fool and followed him out the door.

He walked over to an expensive-looking car, which I assumed was his father's. No sixteen-year-old owns a car like that on a McDonald's salary. Wrong again. This *was* his car. He told me his dad bought it for him but only on condition he worked for the summer.

"My dad owned his own business by the time he was eighteen," he said, as we drove along to I still didn't know where. "He started driving trucks. Then he took out a loan to buy one, and now he owns two hundred of 'em. I plan on owning my own business too. But not in trucking. Computers are the thing now, right?"

I agreed, even though what I knew about computers could be put on the head of a match and burned. I would have agreed with anything he said.

I couldn't believe after all that day-dreaming, I was finally sitting next to him. I was his girl in his car. But I had to admit he looked a lot better from the side than straight on. I'm just the opposite. I have a bit of a double chin. I made sure to stick my chin out to stretch the skin when he turned to look at me, but he didn't look at me too often. He kept his eyes on the road, which was just as well. He was driving a good thirty kilometres over the speed limit.

The speed just added to my crazy euphoria. All I wanted to do was sit next to him in that car and careen down an endless street and have time remain at twilight, a tender dreamy twilight.

We ended up down at a small lake just outside the city limits. I thought we were going to park, and he would try something. I was ready for it. He could try anything he wanted. But he got out of the car, opened the trunk, and took out a fishing pole. He told me to grab the twelve-pack of beer next to it.

We walked to a bridge where the lake narrowed into a river. "This is the best time to fish. Wanna hand me a beer?" he asked, casting his line from the bridge.

"Can I have one too?" I asked

"I didn't bring that many."

That was okay. I didn't need a beer. I didn't need anything. "I used to go fishing when I was little," I said, handing him a beer.

"Oh yeah," he muttered. "Can you pull the cap off for me?"

I pulled the cap off. The beer foamed up through the opening. He put the foaming can to his mouth and took a long drink. It was so sexy. "But guess what happened once when I went fishing," I said, "I was with___"

He interrupted with, "I used to bring Lisa down here. It was great being with her."

The dream ended right there. I pulled out a beer from his pack.

"But she hated fishing," he added. "She thought it was cruel. She thought fish felt a whole lot of pain when they bit into the hook. I told her fish don't have any feelings. Right?"

"Sounds fishy to me," I replied. He laughed. If nothing else, I could make him laugh.

"The problem with Lisa is she's got feelings about *everything*. How can you live like that? You'd go nuts. Hey, you wanna give me another beer?"

I handed him another beer, and he gave me his fishing pole. "Why don't you take over for a bit."

I caught a fish while he was busy drinking the rest of the beer. It was a little sunfish, too small to keep. He yelled at me to be gentle with it. Who did he think I was? Josef Mengele?

I held the fish's quivering little body and tried my best to pull out the hook as tenderly as I could, but a chunk of its lip came off. It gave one last shudder and then became still and flat in my hand. Chester came over and stood next to me as I dropped it back into the water. We both watched it float lifelessly away.

It was probably the beer, but Chester became all teary-eyed. He pulled me close to him for a few moments, and then he kissed me. The kiss felt like listening to Debussy.

He pulled me up a pathway into a small clearing in the woods, and we made out on the grass.

We didn't go all the way because I started crying, which put a real damper on things. We drove home in silence.

Just before I got out of the car, he mumbled something about "maybe next time." He gave me a kiss, but it was more like a kiss-off. I got out of the car. And that was then the end of my glorious date with Chester.

Chapter Seventeen

All the lights were on when I walked towards the house. It was only nine-thirty, and I didn't want to run the gauntlet of Helen and Dan. I turned left and kept walking.

All those long-gone-wrong songs played in my head as I stumbled along. I don't know what made me keep on loving Chester. He made me feel like shit. If only I could find that switch inside me, that needs to love him, and I would turn it off. Why should I love anybody? Love only works out in romantic comedies. My life was a romantic tragedy. So was Mrs. Canyon's. I think she had really loved her husband enough to throw out the piano after he died. But what did love give her? A dead husband and no piano.

I ended up at the park where I met that guy. There was a van parked under some trees at the entrance. Two people were kissing inside it. Well, good luck to you both. Something's sure to happen to send all that passion down the toilet. You poor misguided fools.

The van looked familiar, but then most vans looked the same to me. It looked like Dan's van. It *was* Dan's van. Someone had stolen it to neck in. At last, something passionate was going on inside it. I walked closer. Now I was turning into a *voyeur.* The woman had her hair back in a ponytail. The man was holding it while he kissed her. Whatever turns you on. The man twisted his head so that I could see a bald spot. It looked like Dan's bald spot. Oh, my God, it *was* Dan!

It was so creepy watching someone you thought was as pure as St. Francis of Assisi make out. Even though I had tried to break up their marriage, it wasn't supposed to look like this. It was so seamy. Something just as perverse made me walk right up to the driver's window.

The woman noticed me first. She screamed. Dan turned around. His face was smeared with lipstick. He looked gross. I ran all the way home.

There was no way I could face Helen. I would just sit on the porch steps and wait until she went to bed. Then what? Sooner or later, I had to face her.

I forced myself to view what I had seen in a whole different light. After all, Dan wasn't my father, and Helen certainly wasn't my mother, and she didn't love Dan. She loved Nigel, who made magic glass bowls, but I still thought he was an asshole.

It would be strange if the woman in Dan's car was named Colette. That made me laugh even though it wasn't really funny.

"What're you doing out here?" I heard Helen call from behind me. She must have heard me laughing.

"Nothing." She slammed the door shut. I got up. No sense in hiding the fact that I was there. I went inside. There were suitcases in the hallway. Helen must have found out about Dan. It would be easier to face her now. She was in the kitchen writing a letter.

"You're home early," she said, not looking up from her letter. "You could've stayed away all night if you wanted to. You're a free agent now because I'm leaving." She underscored something on the letter, then signed it with a dramatic flourish. "I can no longer stay with a man I don't love. This is my farewell note to him, and I emphasize the word *note*." She folded the note into a neat square.

"Good luck with your lake swim, but there isn't a chance in hell you'll never make it across." She tucked the note into an envelope. "Although I'd have to admit for a while there, I climbed aboard your fantasy bandwagon too, to take my mind off everything. But you can't take your mind off life. You have to live it." She licked the envelope end to end. "You have to face what you have and what you don't have and make the best of it." She hammered the back of the envelope with her fist.

"Dan wanted to become a hairdresser." Why I said that I'll never know, but it made Helen raise both eyebrows.

"*What?*"

"He told me he wanted to become a hairdresser."

"Dan a hairdresser? That's impossible. Unless he's a latent homosexual. Maybe that's what he is."

"No, he's not gay because...." I suddenly realized that she didn't know about the woman in the van. I had to backtrack. "You don't love him, right?"

"Absolutely."

Sound sounded pretty convincing, so I figured it was okay to continue. "I saw him in his van with another woman." I was wrong. I should have kept my big mouth shut. She took in a sharp breath as if she had been stabbed. "But they weren't doing anything."

"Yes, they were."

No one else could see through me like Helen could. "What was she like?" she tried to sound nonchalant, but I could see through her too.

"I dunno. I didn't get a good look at her."

"Was she white?"

"Yeah."

"How old was she?"

"I dunno. It was hard to tell. I really didn't get a good look."

"What were they doing?"

"They were just___"

"Stop," she said, cutting off another one of my lies in the making. She picked up the envelope and ripped it in half. "It was probably that French slut, Colette."

I should have told her that *I* was Colette, but I didn't. So hang me from the tallest tree.

"Why should I be the one leaving!" She ripped up the envelope until it became a pile of confetti. "This is my *home*! Let *him* leave."

She marched out of the kitchen, and I followed her. She lifted her suitcases from the hallway and carried them up the stairs to her bedroom. I waited in the hallway. A few minutes later she came out of the bedroom with an armful of Dan's clothes, carried them downstairs to the front door, opened it, threw the clothes onto the front porch, slammed the door shut, bolted it, and went back upstairs to her bedroom and slammed that door too.

I was in a real mess now, brought on by my own doing. No matter how hard I tried to convince myself that I hadn't wanted to tell her about that woman, I *had* wanted to tell her. I wanted her to suffer, just like I was suffering. I deserved what lay ahead. If Helen was kicking Dan out, I would be alone with her. That would be punishment enough.

It took me hours to fall asleep, and when I did, I dreamed the Lake had frozen. I could walk across it. That would be so much easier than swimming it. But I wanted to get inside it. I kept pounding on the ice, but it was impenetrable.

I woke up at 10:00 a.m. I'd forgotten to set the alarm. When I called Mrs. Canyon to apologize for sleeping in, she cut me off.

"You'd rather just talk about swimming the lake but aren't the least bit serious about actually getting into the water."

I had to admit that was pretty close to the truth. "No, it's because... I'm moving." That was pretty close to the truth.

"Moving. Where to?"

"I'm not sure. Everything is still up in the air."

"There's a lot of things up in the air. You should not be one of them."

As I hung up the receiver and thought about hanging myself up, I noticed an envelope addressed to me on the kitchen table. There were five ten-dollar bills and a note inside. The note was from Helen. Apparently, she was going away for a week to get her "head straight."

I went outside to the porch and saw that all of Dan's clothes were gone. Normally I was the one to leave a foster home, not the foster parents. It was kind of an exciting situation to be in. Not only did I have my own room, but now I had a whole house, at least until Helen got back.

I made myself breakfast: burnt scrambled eggs and toast. I was just finishing up when the phone rang. It was Lisa.

"What happened to you last night?" she asked.

"A lot of things."

"You said you were coming over, and when you didn't show up or call, I was worried."

I took a deep breath. I would be merciful yet direct. "I went out with Chester." There I said it. Obviously via the safety of the phone and not face-to-face, but I thought this would make her hang up.

"I wouldn't see him anymore if I were you," she said after what seemed like an hour's pause. "He's a real jerk."

Calling somebody a jerk wasn't something I ever expected to hear from Lisa. Maybe I had corrupted her. Maybe she was jealous. Maybe I was turning into a psychopath who needed to rip out everybody's heart.

"I'm a jerk, too," I said.

"No, you're not."

"Yes, I *am*."

"Penny, that's what's wrong with you. You think so little of yourself, but you shouldn't."

"Listen, I don't need you to tell me what's wrong with me. So quit worrying about me and quit calling me all the time!"

"I don't keep calling you all the time. This is only the second time, but if you really don't want me to bother you anymore, I won't."

"Then don't!"

"Okay, if that's the way you want it. Goodbye, Penny, and goodluck with your swim."

I was shaking when I hung up the phone. She made me so furious. She had to be nice about everything. She was like a nun who was so clean she made you feel dirty no matter how hard you tried to scrub your soul. I picked up the phone and called McDonald's. I heard the guy who answered call me something obscene when he hollered for Chester.

"Hi, it's me," I said when Chester finally came to the phone.

"Who?"

"Penny"

"Oh," his voice couldn't have been any flatter.

"I was just thinking____" I began, but he cut me off.

"Listen, they don't like us getting personal calls."

"My folks are away for the week, and I was just wondering if you wanted to come over tonight."

He took a moment to evaluate the proposition. Then I could almost hear his libido kick in. "Okay, but it would be late."

"That's fine – I never sleep," I said and hung up.

I felt a surge of exhilaration, followed instantly by an even stronger surge of self-disgust. I might as well have said, "Come over and fuck me, then throw me in the garbage after you're finished." Which was precisely what was going to happen. I thought about calling him back, but instead, I called Mrs. Canyon. She answered after the tenth ring.

"Mrs. Canyon, we're not moving, and I absolutely have to swim the Lake. Now more than ever."

"What the hell's going on with you?"

"I don't know."

"I can't talk now. Call me later."

"After I lose my virginity." She didn't hear me say that. She had already hung up. There was nothing left for me to do now but wait for Chester to show up and do the job. It was about time I lost my virginity. I would do it without crying. Piece of cake. No, it was a piece of me that would be gone forever. Maybe it might change the whole way I thought about myself. That's what was really wrong with me. I was sexually frustrated. I need to get laid. It would calm me down. I would become serene. Maybe I would become pregnant.

I went upstairs to the bathroom and looked through the medicine cabinet for some safes. I knew Chester wasn't the type to bring any. I found one underneath a crusted bottle of Pepto-Bismol. How in the hell am I going to give him a safe?

I would wait until the moment arrived.

No, that might slow things down. I would leave it somewhere where he'd notice it. Like where? Pasted to my forehead?

What I did next made no sense at all. I took out the safe and blew it up. It expanded into a huge balloon. I could barely squeeze it through the bathroom window.

After setting it free, I watched it sail playfully over the Normans' backyard and over the next one and the next one after that. I laughed hysterically, then closed the bathroom window and went downstairs.

I had to find something else to do to take my mind off what lay ahead. I went into the den and turned on the TV. An old rerun of Columbo was on. I've always had a crush on him. I know he's a fictitious character but so what? I have a whole slew of fictitious lovers: Sydney Carton from *A Tale of Two Cities*, Lord Peter Wimsey from Dorothy Sayers' detective novels, and, of course, Holden Caulfield from *The Catcher In the Rye*. But Columbo outranks them all with his rumpled raincoat, perpetual cigar, and piercing glass eye. I would love to meet him, even if the only way of doing that is to commit murder. I would be thrilled to have him interrogate me in that just about-to-leave-but-comes-back style of his.

Unlike his usual suspects, it would never annoy me. I would encourage it. I would love it. I wish Chester was like Columbo.

The problem was I couldn't even concentrate on *Columbo*. I stood by the living room window and watched the world go by until a tiny meteor hit the glass. That's what I thought it was at first. It turned out to be a sparrow.

I rushed outside and saw this little kamikaze sparrow frozen in stunned surprise on the ground. I carefully placed him in the cup of my hand and went inside.

The sparrow ended up in Nigel's bowl. As soon as he was safely inside the bowl, he rolled over on his side. His tiny chest was pumping so hard I thought he would burst. He reminded me of that sunfish I had killed. I didn't want to watch him die. I ran outside and circled the backyard a few times until I calmed down. I couldn't just leave him alone like that. He would feel pretty weird dying in Nigel's bowl. I would not let him die like that. I would take him outside where he'd feel more at home.

I went back inside and peeked cautiously around the corner of the dining-room door. That sparrow was now standing in the bowl, looking miraculously pert. I wanted to cheer but thought that would scare him. I tiptoed towards him, whispering, "It's okay. It's okay."

The bird gave me a sharp look as if to say, "What the hell am I doing here?"

I should have taken him outside and let him go free, but there was no telling what would happen to him outdoors in his weakened state. I brought in grass and leaves and carefully dropped them into the bowl. All this crap being dumped on him made him flutter crazily. I put my hand over the top of the bow so he wouldn't escape.

Kamikaze (as I had now named him) settled down after a while. In fact, he acted like he was completely at home by rearranging the foliage to suit his style. I sat for a couple of hours watching Kamikaze, and she (I had now decided "he" was a "she") looked very inquisitively at me. We shared life stories. I tried to feed her Corn Flakes, breadcrumbs, and potato chips, a regular buffet of what I thought she would like, but she wouldn't have any of it. She gave me this look, with those little black ball-bearing eyes of hers, as if to say, "what the hell is this crap?"

Maybe she wanted worms. There was no way I was going to get those. But out I went and dug up a big fat one. I dropped it into the blow next to her and said, "*Bon appetit.*" She went berserk at the sight of it, escaped from the bowl, and flew into the living room window. I guess she had hardened herself hitting windows because she bounded off and still kept flying. She flew in a zigzag pattern around the room and out into the vestibule. I opened the front door, and in an instant, she was gone. I burst into tears.

Still crying. I phoned Mrs. Canyon again, but she wasn't home. I called Chester again, but he had already left work. He was on his way over to claim my virginity.

It was turning dark, not only outside but also inside me. I took out a beer from the fridge and guzzled it. I finished three beers this way. I put on my Queen tape and turned the volume up full blast. I danced wildly, jumping on and off the living room furniture. I picked up the crystal bowl Nigel's masterpiece, now filled with the mess of Kamikazes abandoned home, and smashed it on the floor. The sound of it breaking had a delicate ring to it. The doorbell rang too.

I let it ring a few times before I flung open the door. Chester grinned back at me. I smiled as soberly as I could.

"You blasted?" he asked, sauntering past me and into the living room.

"No," I said, weaving behind him.

"So, where are your parents?"

"They're dead.

"Dead?"

"They died when I was seven."

"You mean you've been living here *alone* since you were seven?"

"No, I mean, my real parents died when I was seven. The people I'm staying with now are just my foster parents. I've had a trillion foster parents."

"So you're like adopted?"

"No, I'm like rented."

"Whatta drag."

"Yessirree, it sure is."

"You sure you're not drunk?"

"Yes, and quit asking. Wanna beer?"

"Sure."

Chester followed me to the kitchen via the dining room. "What's this?" he asked, stepping over the remains of the bowl. "You should clean it up."

I handed him a broom and a beer. Here, you do it."

He took the beer but ignored the broom and went back to look at the mess. "What is all this shit?"

"Well, you see there was this bird that flew against the window___"

"You should really clean it up."

"Will you let me finish my fucking story?"

"You *are* bombed, aren't ya."

"So big fucking deal. You won't let me finish anything I try to tell you!"

"Maybe I should leave."

"Fine." I grabbed myself another beer from the fridge.

Chester came into the kitchen and leaned against the fridge while he chug-a-lugged the rest of his beer.

"So finish your story." He said after letting out a big belch.

I told him I had knocked the bowl over when chasing the bird around but left out the crying part. I wasted the lie. He was just pretending to listen.

"So, where are your foster parents now?" he asked, helping himself to another beer.

"On vacation for a week."

"How come you didn't go with them?"

"Would you like to spend a week with your parents at some dumb lodge?"

"We have our own cottage."

"Must be nice."

"It sure is. Plus, we have four boats." He described the boats in minute detail. This time I was the one who pretended to listen. I had two more beers. I was getting really drunk – drunk enough to make me feel I could have sex without crying. I took his hand and led him upstairs. As we passed the bathroom, I made the mistake of looking at the toilet bowl. How romantic.

I didn't know how long I had been in the bathroom – a couple of minutes or maybe a couple of hours – but when I came out, Chester was gone.

That suited me just fine. I would go down to the Lake and jump in. I would get the whole fucking thing over with. That's what everyone wanted, especially the Lake. It just wanted to claim another body. Well, you can have mine, you Big Fucking Asshole of a Lake!

I stopped at the park on the way to my doom. I was hoping Kamikaze might spot me and fly down to wish me farewell, but it was too late for birds to be up. I convinced myself that she was nearby asleep in one of the trees. I fell asleep in my usual spot under the picnic table.

Chapter Eighteen

The next morning I awoke in hell. All I could smell was vomit and beer. Well, at least there was beer in hell. Something was licking my face. I opened my eyes and saw a black angel, Boris, the dog. His barking hit my eardrums like cannonballs. That was just mildly annoying compared with what happened next. I saw Lisa walking towards me with Boris's owner. What the hell was she doing with him? Probably just someone else to rescue.

I crawled out from under the picnic table like a slug. Lisa was more than amazed to see me. "Penny!" she screamed. My eardrums collapsed.

"Are you okay?" the guy asked.

"Yeah...I...I. got home late last night, and my parents locked me out."

"How awful," said Lisa. "How could they do that?"

"Cause they thought I was in already." I looked down and noticed that a dried streak of vomit decorated my T-shirt. It was one of those moments you never want to return to. "Oh, shit, I must've slept on something. I should get home. My parents must be worried about me."

"My brother could drive you home," Lisa offered, gesturing to the guy.

"*Your brother?*" I immediately saw the family resemblance. Why hadn't I seen it before? Oh, no, this could not be happening. Why must I become more entangled in Lisa's life?"

"You're finally going to meet him after all. Tony, this is Penny. Penny, this is Tony. She's the girl I was telling you about who's going to swim Lake Ontario."

Tony's eyes widened with the same childlike amazement that Lisa had. But he didn't hold it as long. "We met before."

"You did?" asked Lisa, doing a triple-take at both Tony and me.

"Yeah, at a park," Tony answered.

I was saved. He had confused me with some other girl. That bothered me a bit. I thought I had made somewhat of an impression on him.

"This time," he said with a wink, "won't you let me drive you home?"

I didn't know what that wink meant. Maybe it was a come-on. Forget it. Tony would be the last guy I wanted to come on to me.

"Sure, she will," Lisa answered for me. "She's in no condition to walk home."

I was just hungover. I could still walk. Besides, how could Lisa recognize a hangover when she saw one? Probably from being with Chester. "I think I'd better walk home. I must smell pretty bad."

"So does Boris," said Tony. "He cancels any other smell around him."

Boris growled at me. I didn't blame him. "I don't think he likes me," I said.

"No," replied Tony, "it's a reverse thing with him. He growls at people he likes."

"Just like you, Penny," Lisa whispered, locking her arm securely around mine. She was thrilled to have me trapped in her kindness.

On the drive home, Lisa did most of the talking, in fact, all of the talking. Tony tried to put a lid on it because all she talked about was how wonderful he was. She sounded more like his agent than his sister.

I heard in boring detail that Tony was in first-year university studying to become a marine biologist: he had been an Eagle Scout; valedictorian of his high-school graduation class; had led the school basketball team to victory by sinking the winning shot; and had once saved a man choking on some meat in a restaurant by performing the Heimlich maneuver on him, which he had learned by taking at St. John's Ambulance Course, which he had passed with flying colours. I guess sainthood ran in Lisa's family.

When we got to the Normans', Lisa stayed in the car while Tony walked me to the door. Obviously, she was trying to set me up with him, which made me feel even more neutral about him, "Well, thanks for driving me home," I said.

"No problem," he said. That "no problem" reminded me of Dan.

I opened the door, but just before I stepped inside, he asked, "Did you ever find your grandmother's ring?"

My insides froze. He *had* remembered how we met. There was a blush to his smile. It helped me tell him the truth. "I've never had a grandmother or a grandmother's ring," I said with unswerving directness to his left foot.

Before he could respond, I was inside with the door closed behind me. He was a nice guy. Too bad he was way too dorky and way too skinny, and Lisa's brother.

I went on a cleaning rampage. I swept up the remains of the crystal bowl and mopped up my vomit from the bathroom floor. I washed, and polished, and vacuumed the house from top to bottom. Helen would have been very impressed, that is up until she found out about Nigel's bowl.

I had a shower and scrubbed my body without mercy, washed my hair four times, and crawled into bed, wet hair and all.

Sleep wasn't about to happen. The silence of the empty house was too deafening. So much for having the place to myself.

I went out for a walk. Around the block, I went, again and again, trying to exhaust myself. Amazingly, something caught my attention: The safe I had released. I discovered it spread limply across the neighbour's hedge. I put the safe back under the Pepto-Bismol bottle in the bathroom, climbed into bed, and was instantly asleep.

I dreamed I was in the Lake. Now all my dreams were about the Lake: it had taken over my subconscious. Pink scaly creatures were closing in on me. Their teeth were as white and even as Chiclets held in placed by blood-red gums. I woke up in a cold sweat. My room was in darkness. In a panic, I reached to turn the lamp on next to me but knocked it to the floor, breaking the bulb. The only light left was from the red numbers on my digital clock. It was 9:00 p.m. I had slept for ten hours.

I went into the bathroom, got in the shower without bothering to take off my clothes, turned the hot water on full blast, got out, slogged my way to the phone, and dialed Lisa's number. None of this made any sense, not even to me.

Lisa answered.

"I just wanted to thank you," I said, "and your brother for driving me home."

"Well, you're welcome, Penny."

"Did he say anything to you?"

"What do you mean?"

"I dunno. I mean anything about...you know...anything."

"You mean about you?"

"Well, that or anything else."

"No."

"Maybe I should thank him; personally, you know, I mean if he's there."

"No, he's not here. He left for up north."

"Up north?"

"Yeah. He got a summer job planting trees up there."

"Trees?"

"Yeah. But I'll tell him you called."

"No, don't bother. I mean___"

"It's no bother."

"I mean, just forget it," I said and hung up. The phone rang seconds afterward. I yanked up the receiver again. "I said forget it, Lisa." But it was Chester.

"What's going on?" he asked.

"Oh, nothing," I stuttered.

"What are you talking to Lisa about? Was she talking about me?" he asked eagerly.

"Yeah, she said you were a jerk."

He just laughed. "Really? "How's, she doin'?"

"Why don't you call her up and ask her yourself." I wanted to hang up, but, of course, I didn't.

"She won't talk to me anymore."

"I don't blame her."

"Look, do you want me to come over again, or what?"

Nothing I said mattered to him at all. "Not really," I said. Why didn't I tell him to fuck off? I was now standing in a puddle of water from my dripping clothes.

"Does that mean yes or no?"

He knew I was helpless. He was enjoying his power over me.

"Why don't we go out somewhere?" If I knew what part of me asked that, I would shoot it and put it out of its misery.

"My dad won't let me use the car."

"I thought it was *your* car?"

"But I told you about the conditions."

"What conditions?"

"I *told* you. Talk about not listening."

"Why don't we just go for a walk?"

"I'll think about it." He hung up.

What a shit. What a fucking shit he was. I could not deal with my rage. It made me so desperate. I called Mrs. Canyon again. There still wasn't any answer.

***

The lights were off when I got to Canyon's house. I rang the bell anyway, but there was no answer. I went to the back porch and sat down. One of her cats joined me, curling its body around my leg. I threw it down the steps. It was only three steps. The cat landed safely and came back up the steps in an instant to annoy me. I thought about strangling it. Instead, I scratched its neck. It started purring. I picked it up and held it close. Its little purring heart comforted me.

I was holding it too tightly. It squirmed out of my arms, trotted down the steps, and disappeared into the night.

Chester would be at the Normans' by now. I hoped he was waiting on my porch for me to show up.

I hoped his yearning for Lisa was just as painful as mine was for him. I wished Tony made me feel about him the way I felt about Chester.

Chapter Nineteen

I slept on Mrs. Canyon's porch without the Lake raising its watery head in my dreams. Mrs. Canyon woke me up. She didn't look surprised to find me, but she was angry in her not really angry way.

"What the hell are you doing here?"

"I'm locked out."

"Don't you have a key to your house?"

"It's not my house."

"What do you mean it's not your house?"

"I mean, there's nobody home at my house."

"Did they move without taking you?"

"Maybe."

"Jesus Christ. When are you going to tell me the truth?"

"I *am* telling you the truth. They left without taking me." I tried to cry, but nothing came out.

"What kind of parents would do that?"

"Mine." This was the complete truth.

She let out a sigh big enough to make her look thinner. "Come on inside, and I'll fix you something to eat."

I didn't want anything to eat. I just wanted to see her, but I would have eaten a dead rat if I had to.

"It's a good thing the lock on the front door is stuck," she said, piling cold cuts onto a slab of bread. "That's usually the way I come in. Otherwise, I wouldn't have found you till morning." She cut into four stacked sandwiches with one strong slice. There must be a lot of muscle under those fleshy arms, but she had the wrong hands attached to them. They looked small and fragile. Their nails were lacquered with pink polish. I had never known her to wear nail polish before. I thought she was too scientific for that.

"I went to a piano recital for my grandnephew," she said, running her pink-tipped fingers through a spray of tap water. "I hadn't heard a piano since Harry passed away. No, he didn't pass away. He dropped dead. That's what he did. I made up a whole pile of excuses for not going to listen to a six-year-old bang out *Song of the Volga Boatmen*, but there are some things you just have to do. Here's your sandwich."

She handed me the stack of sandwiches. The fact that I really hadn't eaten anything in two days finally made it to my brain, "How was it?" I asked with a mouthful of sandwich.

"It wasn't as painful as I thought it was going to be. Now, enough about that. What about you?"

I told Mrs. Canyon all about the Normans, even about Dan wanting to be a hairdresser and my entire life story without a single deception – except the part about Chester. I was too ashamed to talk about him.

"She should not have left you alone. She sounds like she needs a foster parent," said Mrs. Canyon.

"I don't want to be put in another home. I want to find my own."

"You have a whole lifetime ahead of you to do that. But for now, you're stuck with the Normans. Just keep this in mind, though; as long as you keep acting like a rogue wolf, you're going to be treated like one."

I didn't know what "rogue" meant but didn't want to ask. The only thing I had impressed her about in class was my vocabulary. But I figured by the sound of the word, it wasn't complimentary.

"You can stay here tonight."

I was instantly relieved.

She must still like me. Or maybe she was just kind. Maybe I was just another stray cat. "I'll sleep out on the porch."

"See what I mean?" she said, "Stop thinking of yourself that way. You can sleep in the guest room."

What way? I didn't understand what she was talking about, and it wasn't even about physics. All I wanted to do was impress her. "I still want to swim the Lake." I even felt convinced of that myself.

"We'll see about that tomorrow."

Mrs. Canyon's guest room was more like a storage room for books. They lined the walls right up to the ceiling. I've always found books to be the perfect insulator. One shelf had a line-up of dictionaries. I took out the fattest one and looked up "rogue." "Idle vagrant, knave, rascal, swindler...." I skipped down to the end part. "Apart from the herd and of savage temper." My eyes stung with tears. I fought them back. It was the "wolf" part I would hang on to. I've always admired wolves. They're one of the few animals where both parents raise their young.

I picked out a hardcover entitled *The Static of Materials* to take my mind off the whole thing. I fell asleep after the first sentence.

The next morning, I woke up late but still felt really tired. There was something wrong with me. Maybe I had leukemia. I knew a girl who had died from it. She was my age. She lived next door to one of my foster homes. She always had blue circles under her eyes. Just like the ones I saw when I looked into Canyon's bathroom mirror.

I told Mrs. Canyon at breakfast that I had leukemia. I loved the whole idea of it. It would be such a beautifully tragic end to me – plus Mrs. Canyon would no longer think of me as a rogue.

Canyon told me if I had leukemia. I had better start my swimming training before it got any worse. She wasn't exactly the maternal type. She sent me home to get my swimsuit and told me to meet her at the school. She had the key to the pool.

When I got home, Dan was in the kitchen. His back was to me. He was gripping the edge of the sink, staring out at the nothingness of the backyard. He jumped when I said, "Hi."

"Penny, you're still here?"

It was pretty obvious that I was still there, but I was just as surprised as he was, "Yeah, but Helen's not."

"She's *not?*"

"She left to get her hair, I mean, head straight."

"How long is that gonna take?"

"I dunno." We both knew that would never happen.

"She left you here by *yourself?*"

"I'm okay."

"Well, I'll have to stay here till she gets back."

"You don't *have* to."

"Well, I'm gonna. If Mrs. Horshaw found out about you bein' left alone, we'd be in deeper shit than we're already in."

"I'm not exactly a baby."

"You're still under our care, which I guess isn't worth that much, is it."

"It's been okay. I've had worse. Besides, it's been kind of interesting being on my own." That was a bit of an understatement.

"What've you been doing?"

"Nothing much. Just watching TV. But I'm starting my training today."

"Training for what?"

"To swim the Lake."

"Oh, that."

I was used to grown-ups never remembering anything important I had to say, but this time it really hurt. Not only had he not remembered, but he made it sound like it wasn't important. Like it was just my usual bullshit. Well, I wouldn't take him seriously either. Besides, he was a cheat, just like every other male in the universe. "I just came home to get my bathing suit. I'm training at the school's pool."

"I'll drive ya over."

"No, that's okay."

"No, I'll drive ya over."

"No, I'll walk."

"I'll *drive* ya over!"

His anger scared me because I'd never seen it before. Nor did I have the courage to confront it. Instead, I got my stuff together as quickly as possible.

Dan took the longest route to the pool. I think he needed to calm down to a state where he could open up. He started talking after being honked at for not moving after a light had turned green.

"Listen, I'm sorry about what you saw in the van that night. But it's not what you think. Helen and I had a big fight that night after you left. She told me I wasn't worth shit. I knew if I had stayed any longer, I would've slugged her. So, I left. I went to this bar and met an old friend of mine. She had just left her husband. We both needed a shoulder to cry on. Only it must've looked to you like a lot more than that."

It sure did, but I didn't want to hear any more details. Anything about sex is just too embarrassing to hear from a grown-up.

"I'm sorry," he continued. "But I figured I owed you an explanation. I won't' be seeing her anymore."

He should be telling this to Helen. Maybe he could only talk to somebody neutral.

Maybe that's why the Normans wanted me to stay with them. I was their shrink. Well, imagine that. A deranged sixteen-year-old was the Normans' shrink.

We pulled into the school parking lot just as Mrs. Canyon was pulling into it too. Introductions were made, then Mrs. Canyon fired the first round. "Why was she left alone?"

"I didn't know she was left alone," Dan fired back. He didn't scare Canyon. She moved in closer to him.

"Because you were too busy screwing around on your wife."

"She kicked me out!"

There was a monetary cease-fire. Dan retreated into a calmer tone. "Don't' worry, I'm gonna stay with Penny till Helen gets back."

"You should've become a hairdresser." Mrs. Canyon had to go and say that.

I cringed. Dan looked at me like I had betrayed him in the worse possible way. I guess we were even now.

"Did you tell Helen about that too?" he asked.

I shook my head, but I knew he knew I was lying. I waited for the blast, but instead, he lit up into a smile – the kind used to hide embarrassment.

Mrs. Canyon defused everything by taking my hand and tugging me along with her. "We only have the pool for an hour, and we're already late."

Dan followed us. "I think it's great that you're helping her with this...thing."

"And you should be helping her too," said Mrs. Canyon. "Because what I know about marathon swimming could fit in a snake's eye."

"I'll pick you up in an hour," Don hollered after me.

"And don't be late!" Mrs. Canyon hollered back. She always had to have the final word.

As we entered the school, she whispered, "He's a good man but really unsure of himself."

In a way, that's what I thought about him too, but she figured that out after seeing him at his worst. There was no end to the intelligence of Mrs. Canyon.

Coming out of the locker room in my swimsuit. I walked onto the cold tiles of the pool area. Mrs. Canyon was sprawled on a bench, munching on taco chips and reading a *National Geographic* "Start swimming," she commanded through a mouthful of chips.

I thought about diving into the water to impress her, but I was a flop when it came to diving. The last time I dove, I had hit the water horizontally, like a two-by-four. I walked on tiptoes over to the pool's metal ladder and eased myself delicately into the water. It was like moving through ice cubes. I stood in the shallow end, clenching arms against my chest, waiting for my body to quit screaming, "Get the hell out of here!"

"I turned off the heater," Mrs. Canyon yelled. Her voice echoed off the walls like a sonic boom. "So that you'd get used to the temperature of Lake Ontario, and we haven't got all day for you to do that. So, get going."

I had to do it. I held my breath and stretched out both goose-pimpled arms. I started swimming.

Chapter Twenty

I did thirty laps of the pool that morning. It took me an hour to regain my sent of touch. I thought what I had accomplished was worth something until Mrs. Canyon told me that thirty laps was about .0021 of the distance across Lake Ontario. About as much as an ant would do on its first day crossing the Sahara.

"Every journey begins with the first step," she said, trying to cheer me up.

"Yeah, well, I'm not walking. I'm swimming and freezing my ass off." I answered on the other side of the pool and into my towel.

While I was doing every icy lap, Canyon had consumed the entire bag of chips. She had also written out an eight-week schedule. The first four weeks, I could swim all morning in the pool; the next three weeks, I'd do the same in the Credit River to get used to currents and freshwater; and the last week, I'd swim back and forth along the breakwater at Sunnyside Beach to get used to the Lake and vice versa. At the end of the week, we would pick a day to start my swim across Lake Ontario. She put a time limit on that. I had up until the year 3000.

Marilyn Bell had begun her swim at Youngstown, New York, but Mrs. Canyon said that was just because she wanted to be greeted by Canadians. That was a moot point as far as Canyon was concerned. What side I started on didn't matter. It was getting to the other side that did.

What had taken Marilyn Bell seven years to train for, I planned to do in eight weeks. It all made terrific sense.

Dan was waiting for me in his van, with the motor running and all the windows up. That didn't stop Mrs. Canyon. She kept tapping on the driver's window until he had to roll it down. "Think you could cut my hair for me some time?" She wasn't teasing. She really meant it.

Dan revved up again. "I'm *not* a hairdresser. Get it?"

"How much do you charge?" Dan rolled the window back up. She turned to me. "See you tomorrow, Penny. Same time, same situation."

I climbed into the van. Dan drove off before I could get the door closed.

I have two approaches when I'm in a dicey situation: either I clam up or become a talking hurricane. During the drive home with Dan, I chose the latter. "I'm sorry about telling her about you wanting to be a hairdresser, but I didn't tell Helen. Well, as a matter of fact, I did tell her. I mean, there's one thing you should know about me, I can never keep a secret, and I lie all the time. Well, not all the time, only when I'm cornered, well...even when I'm not cornered. So don't' tell me any more secrets because I'll never keep them.

"Besides, you shouldn't be telling me anything that's a secret between you and Helen. You should be telling Helen. I know she's crazy, but she's not that crazy. I mean, what is *crazy?* I'll tell you what's crazy. What's crazy is trying to act normal when what you have to do to act normal is not normal for you. I think normal is normal only when you feel it's normal. And I'm not saying 'think' I'm saying 'feel.'"I stopped to take a breath, giving Dan an opportunity to say something.

"You're pretty amazin' Penny."

"What do you mean 'pretty amazing'? Like a total eclipse or like a psychopath?"

"I mean, you're pretty amazing."

"You mean like I'm crazy?"

"No, I mean you're amazing in a wonderful way."

What a big fat corny thing to say. It was too big a thing for him, or anybody else, to say to me just like that. It made me feel like crying. I kept quiet for the rest of the drive.

When we walked through the dining room, I was just about to tell him about the crystal bowl, but he got me off that hook.

"I guess she took the bowl with her. Which suits me fine. It gave me the creeps. Let's have a barbecue."

I made a salad, and he made some burgers. Everything was sailing along fine until he asked the inevitable. "Did you drink all that beer?" He was more astonished than angry.

"No." To change the subject, I pretended to cut my finger while slicing a tomato. He wasn't about to change the subject.

"Who did then?"

"Lisa."

"Lisa? Who's Lisa?"

"That girl who visited me last week."

"Her? She didn't look like she had a big enough tank to drink all the beer."

"Well, not usually...she was just____

"Is this straight?"

"Not really."

"So, both of you drank it?"

"Yeah, but she had more than I did."

"You and her shouldn't' be drinkin' that much beer at your age. 'Course I shouldn't be drinkin' that much at my age either. Let's have some of Helen's diet-free-caffeine-free-taste-free cola."

"Why did you marry her?" Even I wasn't prepared for that question. But Dan answered immediately.

"Because I loved her."

"Loved? Like in the past tense?"

"Well, after a while, you don't know what it is anymore. But whatever it is, it sure takes a lot of work. She just never got over losing that baby. It was all she had left of Nigel."

"You *know* about Nigel?"

"Sure I do. She told me everything. I thought she'd get over him, but it doesn't look that way."

"I know how she feels. It's called waiting in line for love, but the person you're waiting for is usually waiting in line for someone or something else, et cetera, et cetera. So, who's at the end of that big love line-up? God?"

"I guess so."

"I don't believe in God, except for the one on the ceiling of the Sistine Chapel."

"The what?"

"It's a painting done by Michelangelo."

"Don't think I've never heard of him, 'cause I have," he insisted. "I know as much about that art stuff as a man like me needs to. 'Course it was never enough for Helen."

"Did you ever want a child of your own?"

"Sure. Still do. But Helen didn't want any more kids...I mean of her own."

"So, you just wanted to rent a ready-made one for a while?"

"That's a crummy way of putting it, but it's pretty close to the truth. We thought havin' a kid around might bring us closer together, but nothing is ever gonna do that. I'm sorry you got caught in the middle. You deserve better."

"What's going to happen now?"

"You wanna leave?"

"I was going to ask you the same question."

"Helen doesn't want me to stay."

"Well, I can't stay here *alone* with her. Can I stay with you?"

"I'll be living in a motel for a while. I don't think Mrs. Horshaw would go along with you stayin' with me in that situation."

"Well, then, after you find a place, can I stay with you?"

"Sure. No problem."

We went outside, and Dan set up the barbecue. While watching his repeated attempts to light the coals, I officially claimed him as my dad. The coals were only partially lit when he threw the burgers on.

We left them unattended. We were too busy talking about this, and that, just easy talk, the kind that I'm sure normal daughters have with normal fathers.

The burgers burned into little black balls. We threw them over the fence. The dog next door had been anxiously waiting for them. We ordered a pizza. Dan let me pick all the toppings.

By the time we had finished the pizza, we were all talked out. Dan watched a Blue Jays game on TV, and I went up to my room.

I lay on my bed and listen to good old Freddie Mercury again. For just one moment before I fell asleep, I experienced the sense of harmony I had felt that day under that tree when watching that otter and listening to that Italian lady watering her flowers.

I fell asleep, and my dreams returned to the Lake. The Sistine Chapel was completely submerged in it. Freddie Mercury was swimming along next to me. We circled each other like two playful otters until God's finger started poking me. It woke me up.

Dan was standing over my bed. "Sorry to wake you," he said, "but there's a guy outside real anxious to see you."

Chapter Twenty-One

Chester was kneeling on the grass barfing his guts out when I came out to the porch.

"I was gonna call the police, but he started bawlin'. You know this guy?" Dan asked with a protective arm around my shoulder.

"Sort of."

Chester finished his last heave and rolled over onto his back. Dan didn't want me to go near Chester, but I assured him that it was okay,

My beloved Chester had cried over me. I wanted to hold him. I would ease all his pain. I knelt down beside him and whispered, "I'm with you now, and I'll never let you go."

His eyes were all glassy and unfocused. He moaned something. At first, it was inaudible, then it became brutally apparent. "Lisa. Lisa."

"Everything okay?" Dan called from the porch.

"No, call the police," I answered. This time, I would not let the pain overwhelm me. I walked steadily back to the porch. Dan somehow knew what had happened because he just stepped aside in respectful silence to let me pass into the house.

I would go back to my Lake dream with Freddie Mercury. I put on my headset and listened to the entire Queen album four times. This was supposed to put me to sleep, but it just gave me a headache. Stumbling down the hallway to grab some pills from the bathroom, I heard the faint sound of a downstairs conversation. I tiptoed over to the top of the stairs to listen.

"My dad was like that too," I heard Dan say. "But you gotta be your own man. Don't let him make you somethin' you're not."

"Yeah, right," said Chester. "No way I'm gonna turn out like the asshole he is."

Obviously, even Dan wasn't immune to Chester's charm. I would march right down there and tell Chester to get the hell out, but I had to eavesdrop first.

"He ain't an asshole," said Dan. "He just ain't you, and you ain't him. I never told anyone this before, but the only reason I became a plumber was because that's what my dad wanted me to be. I wanted to be a fuckin' hairdresser."

"Shit, man, a hairdresser?"

"And I'm not even gay."

"That's fuckin impossible."

"Yeah, well, look at Vee-dal Sassoon, one of the best hairdressers in the world, and he ain't gay."

"You got any more beer?"

"Penny and Lisa drank it all."

"No fuckin' way, man. Lisa doesn't drink. She's a fuckin' angel."

"Maybe this is a different Lisa."

"Listen, I knew you're Penny's like foster parent, but—"

Now was the time to charge down there, but I had waited too long. They'd know I had been eavesdropping.

"Yeah, I know she's got a problem with telling the truth," said Dan.

"She's gotta problem about everything."

"And you're one of them."

"Me? I think she's...."

Chester's voice lowered to a mumble, which went on for a couple of minutes, and then I heard Dan's.

"I think you should just go home and sleep it off. I'll drive ya." This was followed by Chester muttering. Then I heard the front door open and close, and then there was silence.

From my bedroom window, I watched Dan open the van door. Chester stumbled towards it and then stopped. He swayed a bit. Dan caught him before he hit the ground. Then I saw something incredible. Chester put his arms around Dan. Chester was crying. I couldn't watch anymore.

Chapter Twenty-Two

When the alarm went off the next morning, pulling my body out of bed was like pulling it out of quicksand. I had the coldest shower I could stand to prepare myself for what lay ahead: swimming in that arctic pool with a broken heart.

When I finally made it downstairs, Dan was in the kitchen making coffee. "Ready to go?"

I just nodded. I was dying to talk about Chester, but I didn't.

Mrs. Canyon was waiting by her car when we pulled into the parking lot. Dan stayed in the van. One confrontation with Mrs. Canyon was enough for him.

That cold shower had toughened my nerve ends. It took only a few seconds for me to get used to the pool water. My body felt energized, like some dormant molecules that were part of me were suddenly awakened. If I stayed in long enough, I would grow fins and remain in this wonderful state forever. Maybe I am really more fish than human. Why did we humans ever leave the water in the first place? Why can't we be more like otters? They're completely at home in and out of the water. Or like loons? They can walk, swim and fly.

Why can't Chester love me?

Why am I always asking questions that I can never find the answer to?

That day I swam forty laps of the pool.

Chapter Twenty-Three

The rest of the week went by pretty uneventfully, except that the number of laps I swam steadily increased. Dan would take me to the pool in the morning, and Canyon would drive me home when we finished. Dan would make supper, and we'd eat in silence. Then he'd watch TV, and I would go to my room and listen to Freddie Mercury and think about Chester. I'm always wary of an uneventful chain of events. They're like ticking bombs.

Helen came home on Sunday night just after we had finished dinner. She certainly wasn't the same Helen. Her hair was braided in cornrows, and her ears were pierced with shiny gold hoops. She looked radiant and blacker than I'd ever noticed before. I just stared at her with my mouth open. She told Dan to get out. Dan stared at her like he had just fallen in love again. The look on his face made Helen reconsider. She told him he could stay the night on the couch but had to leave in the morning.

After she retreated to her bedroom, I told Dan that if he left, I would too. Dan assured me that Helen would change her mind in the morning and that everything would be back to normal abnormality. I wanted to talk about how she looked, but Dan told me that was Helen's business, not mine.

In the morning, Helen came into the kitchen when Dad and I were having coffee. She looked ready for another round, but before she could say anything, I was up on my feet like a referee.

Maybe it was all that swimming that empowered me because I told them that if they didn't work things out by the time I got back from swimming, I was definitely leaving. I walked to the pool that morning.

When I got back in the afternoon, Dan had left. Helen told me he was gone for good. Of course, I didn't go anywhere except to my room. Me and my big stands. I found a card printed with the name and address of the motel Dan was staying at. There was a note on the back.

"Call me if you need me. Love, Dan." I took a pen and changed the "n" in his name to a "d." I still had hopes that once Dan got moved into a permanent place, he would send for me.

Helen called me for dinner. I told her I wasn't hungry. She brought the dinner up to my room.

"I have to talk to you," she said, putting the tray of food down next to my bed. I knew that room service was just an excuse – she had something she wanted to unload on me. "I went to see Nigel," she explained, "but he's not the man I thought he was. He's totally self-centered. He used to go on and on about how his art would benefit humanity, but all he's really interested in is how his art will benefit him! He talked for about three hours on how he got this rich bitch to pay three times for an ashtray of his than what he had originally asked for. Can you imagine spending that much time on something in which to stub your cigarette? Can you imagine an artist even making an ashtray - something that is only useful to smokers! People that pollute the air with their foul habit! A habit that creates cancer!"

I felt an overpowering urge to have a cigarette.

"He is completely shallow," she continued.

"What man isn't?" I asked.

"You're absolutely right. I have decided to live my life without a man. I think you'd be better off without one too."

"Maybe we could be nuns."

"Nuns become brides of Christ. They are still involved with a man, so to speak."

"Dan wasn't fooling around on you."

"There you go again, Penny. Not listening to a single thing I'm telling you. I don't care about whether he's fooling around or not. I don't care about him. I don't care about any man. That is finished." She picked up the tray of food. I tensed up, waiting for it to be hurled against the wall. "I am liberated from all that." The tray shook in her hands. "I am truly free! You're too young to understand what love is all about. When you're young, it's all so glorious, but it ends up being very, very...I can't think of the right word just yet, but love ends up being just the opposite of glorious."

"Unglorious?"

"You'll never be a writer, Penny if *unglorious* is the only antonym you can come up with for glorious."

"Who said I wanted to be a writer?"

"Right. You want to be a marathon swimmer."

"No, I just want to swim Lake Ontario. That doesn't mean I want to become a marathon swimmer,"

"Then what do you want to become?"

"I want to become an antonym."

"An Opposite?"

"Yeah."

"You don't know one fucking thing about being opposite. Not one fucking thing!" The tray of food went sailing across the room and hit the wall. I wasn't the least bit tense anymore. Maybe I was beginning to understand female rage. We express it by smashing things we use to nurture.

Helen marched out, returning sixty seconds later. "What a terrible shame it is to waste food." She cleaned up the mess and left.

I think Helen was in the early, or middle, or last stages of insanity. Maybe I was too.

Chapter Twenty-four

Helen woke me with her usual timing: five minutes before my alarm went off. She said it was now her responsibility to get me to the pool on time, and she wanted to meet Mrs. Canyon to see for herself how fit she was to be a swimming coach. I was actually looking forward to Helen and Mrs. Canyon meeting.

"You're black," said Mrs. Canyon after I introduced them. "You're white," said Helen.

They were both smiling at each other, but you'd need a sledgehammer to break the tension between them.

"What are your qualifications?" asked Helen.

"What are your qualifications for asking me what mine are?" Mrs. Canyon countered.

Now the gloves were off.

"I beg your pardon," said Helen.

"I'd say you're not qualified to do anything," said Mrs. Canyon. "Why did you leave a sixteen-year-old girl to fend for herself?"

"That is none of your business," Helen shot back. "And if you know so much about looking after sixteen-year-old girls, then why don't you look after her?"

"Because she doesn't want me to be her mother," replied Mrs. Canyon. "She wants you to be that." I had really been enjoying their showdown up until that point, but Mrs. Canyon had gone way over the line. I'd rather have Lucrezia Borgia as my mother than Helen.

"No, she doesn't," said Helen. "This child's heart has been turned to stone because of the way she was treated. She doesn't want a mother's love, or anyone else's for that matter and—"

"You're talking about yourself, not her," said Mrs. Canyon. "And I've already heard about as much as I want to hear from you right now. We've already used up five minutes of Penny's swimming time."

"As long as she's in my care," said Helen, "I will not leave her alone with someone like you!"

"Then come join us," said Mrs. Canyon. She turned around and headed for the school.

I followed her, and Helen followed me.

When I came out of the locker room, Helen and Mrs. Canyon were sitting at opposite ends of the pool, like opposing political parties.

That morning I swam sixty-five lengths.

When the three of us were back in the parking lot, Mrs. Canyon said she was pushing the schedule forward. Tomorrow I would start my training in the Credit River.

"May I talk with you privately?" Helen asked.

"No," replied Mrs. Canyon.

"All right," said Helen. "Then I'll have to say what concerns me in front of her."

"Yes," said Mrs. Canyon, "why not say it in front of her?"

"I think it's wonderful," said Helen, "that she's taking swimming lessons from you—"

"These aren't swimming lessons. She already knows how to swim, but she wants to swim Lake Ontario."

"And I think that's wonderful too," Helen continued, "but we both know that that would be impossible, and I think it's about time somebody around here faced that fact once and for all. Now, it's fine that she comes here every day and swims; she could spend her summer vacation doing far worse things. But carrying this thing any further by making her swim in a polluted river is both cruel and dangerous. And as her guardian, I will not allow it."

"Well," said Mrs. Canyon looking directly at me, "What do you have to say about that?"

"I dunno," I answered without flinching. I was standing between two volcanoes. No matter what I said, one of them was sure to erupt.

"If you continue this, I'll have to call Mrs. Hornshaw," said Helen.

That did it. That was all I needed to hear to give me some backbone.

"Fine," I replied, "and I'll tell her about you leaving me alone for a week."

"Hold it right there," said Canyon. "I'll not be a party to blackmail or any other kind of intimidation. I'll only take part in something that someone wants to do that's impossible."

"Oh, that makes incredible sense," said Helen.

"It sure does," said Mrs. Canyon. "There was a time when electric light was considered impossible. But Thomas Edison didn't think it was. So just think of Penny swimming the Lake the way Edison thought about electric light. I'll pick you up tomorrow at five a.m.,Penny."

Helen didn't say a word on the drive home, but she made this astonishing announcement at dinner that night. "I think you've picked the right coach for your swim. I don't like her, but at least I know where I stand with her. She's not a hypocrite, Penelope."

"*Penelope?*" I said. "My name is Penny."

"Well, it's about time you stopped calling yourself that. Calling yourself *Penny* is just another way of minimizing yourself, whereas *Penelope,* your true namesake, was a Princess of Ancient Greece, the wife of Ulysses. While Ulysses was away on his odyssey, she had one hundred and eight suitors vying for her affection. She turned them all down and waited for Ulysses to return. He was gone for twenty years."

"So what?" It was amazing how I was no longer afraid of saying what I wanted to her. "What does that make her?"

"It makes her extremely loyal."

"Loyal to a man. I thought you said we should be liberated from men."

Helen looked cornered. "I'm not talking about whom she is loyal to. I'm talking about loyalty, period. Loyalty is a very rare commodity these days."

I knew she was talking about Dan. But I also knew that if I brought that up, she would figure out a way to get out of that corner too.

I didn't, however, have to worry about carrying on this debate any further because just then, the phone rang. We both jumped at the sound, although neither of us made a move to answer it.

"It's probably Dan," said Helen after the fourth ring.

I picked up the receiver.

"Hello, is Penny there?" It was a male voice I didn't recognize.

"This is Penny," I said, looking at Helen, who couldn't hide her hopes that it was Dan. I shook my head. She smirked back at me and left the room.

"Hi, Penny," said the caller. "This is Tony, Lisa's brother. She told me you called and wanted to speak to me."

"She did?" There was a charge of static on the line. I could hear Tony's voice intermittently through the crackling interference.

"I'm calling...north...phone booth...." Then there was a break in the static. I could hear him clearly again. "I knew you didn't really lose your grandmother's ring the first time you told me. I've done stuff like that too." Static once more broke up the line. "I want you to know___" And then the line went dead.

What a strange guy.

Helen came sailing back into the room. "It's about time I listened to my true calling," she said, "I'm going to write a novel. I thought I could only do it if I stayed with Nigel. However, you can't depend on anyone to do what you must do for yourself. You must depend on yourself. You must do it yourself. I'm going to start to work right now. The dining room will be where I create. So, until I'm finished, that room is off-limits to you and anyone else. Is that clear?"

"Yes." If she had said she would be crowned the Queen of England, I would have agreed with that too. My only concern was how she would react about Nigel's bowl. There's no way she wouldn't notice it missing. It was about time I came clean.

Helen marched into the dining room like it was a brave new frontier. I remained at the doorway. "Something happened to Nigel's bowl," I said.

"Yes, Dan told me all about it."

"He did?" How did Dan know what had happened?

"He told me he broke it," she said. "I always knew he was extremely jealous of Nigel, but, of course, that doesn't matter now. I don't' care about him or Nigel or Nigel's bowl."

I should have let Dan take the rap for what I had done, but I will always hold onto what I did next as the most, and probably the last, honourable thing I will ever do. I told her the entire truth about the bird and the nest but left out the Chester part.

"Well, in a way, I'm a little disappointed that it wasn't Dan," she said.

So much for her stand on men, so much for mine too. She was going to use my story about the bird "to jump into" her novel.

I wished her luck and went out for a walk.

Of course, I ended up at McDonald's. I saw Chester through the window at his station.

Something made me change my mind about going in, though, and the same something made me head over to Lisa's house.

Chapter Twenty-Five

There was a lawnmower parked on a patch of cut grass on the front lawn of Lisa's house. The grass surrounding it was about half a metre high. The person mowing must have thought finishing the job wasn't worth the effort, or maybe they were called away to something more important, or got struck by lightning, or beamed up by aliens. My imagination always goes overboard when I see things like that abandoned lawnmower.

After I knocked, then pressed the doorbell nonstop, someone finally opened the door – a woman wrapped in a red satin kimono pockmarked with burn scars. Her hair was a semi-bleached blond, and there were half-moon mascara smudges under the eyes. Nevertheless, there was still a lingering beauty about her face.

"You tryin' to wake the dead?" Her breath smelled like stale whiskey. I was hesitant, but the corner of her mouth curled up into something of a smile.

"Is Lisa here?"

"She's out at the store. Come on in, honey. She'll be back in a few minutes."

Leaving the door open, she sashayed down the hallway bumping against the walls a few times. This was Lisa's mother? I was expecting her to be more like Betty Crocker, not Bette Davis. I followed her down the hallway. She disappeared around the kitchen corner, giving me a chance to check out the front room. Compared with the outside, it was trim and orderly. The furnishings were like a museum layout of the fifties. Even the TV looked black and white.

Lisa's mother picked up a lit cigarette from an ashtray on the kitchen table. Her hand trembled as she poked the cigarette into her mouth. Next to the ashtray was a crossword puzzled torn from a newspaper. It was half-finished, done in ink – the true mark of someone who doesn't give a shit about erasing mistakes. Next to the puzzle was a tumbler filled with ice and a liquid that might have been apple juice, but I'm sure it wasn't. She took a drag from her cigarette. The smoke made her eyes narrow, or maybe she was just suspicious. "So, you're a friend of Lisa's or what?"

"Sort of."

"She doesn't have many friends. In fact, she has no friends. How come you don't find her a pain in the ass?"

"I dunno," I said with my usual eloquence. If Lisa was more like her mother, I'd be her friend in a minute.

"You want some pop or something?" She picked up the tumbler and swirled it around. The ice cubes crashed against themselves. It reminded me of that scene with Liz Taylor in *Who's Afraid of Virginia Woolf?*

"No Thanks."

She took a dainty sip of her drink then wiped the corners of her mouth with her thumb and index finger. "I'm Lisa's mother."

It sounded like an apology.

"But please don't call me Mrs. McIver. I consider you my peer, so there's no need for that formality. My name is Dorothy. What's yours?"

"Penny."

"Penny what?"

"Just Penny."

"Penny? You must be worth more than that. Why don't you sit down?"

I sat down, and she picked up her pen and started working on her crossword puzzle. "This is my job – doing crossword puzzles."

"Oh, really?"

"I mean, I don't just do them. I write them. It's my little contribution to civilization. Life on this planet would come to a grinding halt without puzzles, don't you think?" She continued, not waiting or caring for an answer. "I used to be an editor, but I drink too much to do that anymore."

As if on cue, Lisa appeared in the doorway toting two plastic bags of groceries. "Penny!" she screamed.

Why couldn't she ever say my name without screaming it?

"How wonderful to see you!"

"Doesn't she sound like a character right out of Jane Austen?" Dorothy asked, "Don't misinterpret what I'm saying. I love Jane Austen, but this is the twenty-first century."

Lisa forced a laugh and went into action without the least bit of intervention from her mother. She dumped the drink into the sink, stubbed out the cigarette opened the kitchen window, waved out the smoke, and unpacked the groceries. All in less than a few minutes.

"You're just in time for dinner," Lisa said. "I'm making crunchy tuna casserole and a tossed salad. Do you like tuna? Don't worry if you don't because I could make something else."

"How about lobster thermidor?" asked Dorothy.

Lisa smirked back at her

"Thanks, but I've already had my dinner," I said.

"So, have I," Dorothy added. "Why don't you take Penny into the living room and let me get some work done."

"What did you have for dinner?" Lisa asked, with an arched eyebrow.

"I forget, but I'm not hungry." There was enough rebellion in Dorothy's voice to make Lisa back off

"All right. But no more you-know-whats," said Lisa, as if she was talking to a two-year-old.

"Yes, dear," Dorothy answered, rolling her eyes at me with strained forbearance,

Lisa and I headed into the living room, but she made a sharp turn into the vestibule. "Why don't we go to my room?" she whispered. "We can talk better up there."

"You can talk about me anywhere you want!" Dorothy bellowed from the kitchen, "I don't mind."

This time Lisa rolled her eyes,

Lisa's room was a zoo of stuffed animals. They were lined up across her bed against the pillow, in bookcases, on her dresser, on her night table, and piled into all four corners of the room.

"As you can see, I have a few stiff animals."

She was oblivious of the understatement.

"I've been collecting them ever since Ross, our dog, died. He was hit by a car. I saw it happen. Tony forgot to tie Ross up, and he followed me to school. I didn't know Ross was behind me until I heard the brakes of the car. I decided from that day on that I would never own another dog. It's just too cruel to keep them in the city when they could be massacred by a car."

"What about Boris?"

"Boris isn't our dog," she said. "He's our neighbor's. Tony just uses him. He just can't live without taking Boris for a walk."

"He called me."

"Who? Boris?" She immediately cupped her hand to her mouth as if to push back her question. "I meant to say Tony. I don't know why Boris came out. I'm sorry. I'm usually very, very sensible. But I'm just so glad you came over. I'm very sorry. Are you sure you don't want to stay for dinner?"

"Yeah, I'm sure."

"Oh, that's right. You said you had dinner. Wait a minute. Let's start over. You said that Tony called you?"

"Yeah."

"And?"

"And I told ...well, I didn't mean for him to...I mean." Now I was getting all tangled up in what I wanted to say.

"You like him, don't you?" Lisa said, quietly thrilled.

I just nodded.

"He's never called a girl up before, and he's eighteen years old. I think it has something to do with him feeling responsible for our dog being flattened under the wheels of that car. He was fourteen when it happened. I've been working on him ever since, and it's just splendid that all my work has finally paid off."

"I like Tony, but I don't think___"

"Oh, you don't have to go out with him if you don't want to. You can just be friends. Just like we are, right?"

There was nothing to do but agree with her. Maybe I even meant it.

"Would you like to hear my *Phantom of the Opera* tape? I just love Andrew Lloyd Webber."

How could I be friends with someone who loved or even remotely liked Andrew Lloyd Webber? It was just a stone from the mountain of differences between us, "No thinks."

"Chester doesn't like him either." She paused for one cautious moment. "Are you still seeing him?"

"No." That was partly true.

"That's good. He doesn't care about anyone except himself. He tried to take advantage of me."

"What do you mean?"

"I mean, you know what some guys try and do."

"You mean he tried to rape you?"

"No, but he was leading up to that."

"Did this take place at the back of McDonald's?"

"Yes. How did you know?"

"Because I saw you and him."

"Oh, my God. You saw us kissing?"

It sounded like you'd think I'd seen her giving him a blowjob.

"It wasn't exactly a private location, you know."

"But that's what I mean. Kissing someone is a very intimate, private thing, and he didn't care about that. He didn't care how embarrassed I was. He has absolutely no control over himself. He just grabbed me and kissed me on the mouth...on the neck, which in some ways is an even more private place than the mouth."

"Was he sober?' I hoped the answer would be no.

"Yes."

Oh, how I would have loved it if Chester had kissed me that way. "Well," I said, "if you're in love with someone, sometimes you just can't control what you do." Little did she know.

"He's not in love with me." That slipped out without a trace of concern.

"Believe me. I know for sure he's in love with you."

"What do you mean?"

Thank God there was a knock on the bedroom door.

"Lisa, honey," came Dorothy's wobbly voice from the hallway. "I'm goin' for a walk."

Lisa bolted to the door." She's just going to a bar. I have to stop her."

From the bedroom window, I watched Lisa and Dorothy, now dressed in tights, spiked heels, and a zebra-print sweater, out on the sidewalk. Lisa was gripping her mother's arm. Dorothy shook it free and staggered across the street. Lisa went after her.

As I watched them, I felt eyes watching me. When I turned around, every plastic eye of Lisa's stuffed menagerie was fixed on me. If I stayed there any longer, I might end up getting stuffed too.

On the way, out I saw a picture of Lisa and Tony and their departed dog. Lisa was in the middle, with her arms wrapped protectively around them both. I'm sure I saw a ring of gold light hovering over her head.

Lisa and Dorothy had vanished when I got outside.

It took me over an hour, but I finished mowing the lawn. It was about time somebody did something for Lisa.

Chapter Twenty-Six

The dining room looked like it had been struck by a paper blizzard. Tight balls of paper were hurled about helter-skelter. Helen sat at the table, resting her head against an Olivetti. "I started to write my novel, but then I decided it was more of a short story. Then I thought that was even too long, so I decided to write a poem. But now it's boiled down to the first word, but I can't even come up with that."

"What about 'the?" I said. "That's always a good word to start with."

"*The* what? What follows *the*?"

"Whatever you it want."

"I don't know what it wants."

"What's it?"

"What I'm trying to write?"

"Why don't you just sleep on it."

"No, not until I find that word."

"Well, when you've finished whatever you are writing, I know a good editor for you."

"Who?"

"Mrs. McIver."

"Who's she."

"Lisa's mother. She used to be an editor."

"Used to be? And who's Lisa? Oh, never mind. It doesn't matter. I'll never finish it."

I didn't tell her that Mrs. McIver wouldn't be up to editing her book, ever. I figured Helen didn't need to know that until she had finished it.

***

The next morning the alarm went off without Helen waking me beforehand. She was downstairs asleep with her head pressed against the typewriter. I tiptoed over. The page curled around the roller was blank. The lines of her scalp between the cornrows were like little rivers running down her head. I tiptoed out.

No sooner was I on the porch when Mrs. Canyon drove up with a small motorboat hitched on a trailer.

"Where'd you get the boat?" I asked, climbing into the passenger seat.

"Never mind. Where's Helen?"

"Working on her novel."

"Well, I guess if electric light is possible, so is Helen writing a novel."

As we drove along, it suddenly occurred to me that my reason for wanting to swim the Lake had changed. It was no longer to get over Chester. But what was it for? Why did Marilyn Bell do it? For Gus Ryder? He had been a champion of crippled kids. Was Marilyn crippled in an invisible way? But that book made her sound completely normal. Maybe it left out stuff that would make her sound weird. Some day I would ask her.

It took us a while to get the boat into the river, never mind me. Mrs. Canyon insisted she was an able captain. But for the first time, I wasn't sure whether to trust her.

When we finally slid the board into the water, Helen appeared. She was putting aside her duty as a writer because her duty as my foster parent came first. Oh, yeah? Maybe it was more like she couldn't stand her duty as a writer and just needed an excuse to get away from it.

We all piled into the boat. It took Mrs. Canyon fourteen mighty yanks to get the motor started. Helen enjoyed every moment of it. We finally left the safety of the shore. Mrs. Canyon had trouble steering. We went into dizzy circles, much to the entertainment of some kids on the shore. Helen demanded to take over the helm. Canyon told her to back off. Only she didn't use the word "back."

Eventually, Canyon became more of a captain of her ship. We were now in the middle of the river with the boat pointed steadily in the right direction. It was time for me to jump in. Canyon made me coat myself with Vaseline and lanolin. She said all marathon swimmers greased up to protect against heat loss. It was the first time she called me a *marathon* swimmer. I slipped over the side of the boat and into the Credit River. The water was even colder than the pool water, and it sure didn't smell of chlorine. I was determined not to think about what it smelled like. I guess pollution hadn't been invented when Marilyn swam in this river,

I made good time - fifty beats to the minute – just like Marilyn swam. Mrs. Canyon kept the boat about three meters behind me. Helen kept yelling, "Are you all right? Are you all right?" Why couldn't she show that concern when I was on dry land? I was doing just fine – until the cramp hit

My intestines felt like they were being strangled. My mouth opened and filled with scummy river water. I couldn't cry for help. The water was choking me. I heard Helen call me name just before I went under. I curled into a fetal position. The pain had total control over me. I sunk like a dead weight. The water felt warmer and warmer. It eased my tension. All the pain was lulled away. Nothing mattered in this soothing warmth. Drowning was the ultimate serenity. I would stay with it forever. I opened my eyes, expecting to see the meaning of life but felt a sharp pain. Something had grabbed a hunk of my hair and was pulling me upwards. I fought it but couldn't get free. The water was becoming colder. I hated the feeling of it. I grabbed hold of the thing pulling me through this icy hell. It was a hand. The warmth of it made me hold on. I held onto this hand for dear life.

Helen and I broke the surface gasping for air. Canyon almost ran us over with the boat. She maneuvered it around back to us and pulled me up into the boat like I was weightless. She did the same for Helen.

No one said a word until after I vomited up a few liters of river water on the shore.

"Do you need to go to the hospital?" asked Mrs. Canyon. I shook my head. Helen was standing over me, shivering in her wet dress. Mrs. Canyon wrapped a blanket around her. "What about you? You okay?" Helen just nodded. All you could hear was her teeth chattering.

"Thank God you were in the boat, Helen. I can't swim." Then she and Helen began to cry.

Canyon crying? I couldn't bear to watch it. I just wanted to go home. "I'm never going in the water again."

"We'll see about that," said Mrs. Canyon, grabbing a bunch of her dress to wipe her tears with,

"You have to get right back up on the horse after you're thrown," said Helen.

That was strange. She was the one who didn't want me swimming in the river in the first place. Now she would hold saving me over my head forever. It wasn't the same way I had saved her life. There's a big difference between dialing 911 and jumping into a freezing polluted river. Out came the tears. It was so embarrassing – the first time I had ever cried in front of anyone, least of all Helen. She hugged me. It was an awkward hug, and it kept on being awkward, but we got through it.

Canyon pulled a dress out of a bag from her car. It was printed with the usual riot of flowers. She handed it to Helen. "You change into this, and I'll unpack the lunch,' she said. Helen looked at the dress like she wouldn't be caught dead in it but put it on anyway.

I thought my stomach would never be ready for food again. However, I ate half the roast chicken, some pasta salad and vegetable salad, a few rolls, four chocolate-chip cookies, and some watermelon. Helen and Mrs. Canyon didn't eat anything. That wasn't strange for

Helen; she ate like a bird most of the time. But I thought Canyon had an appetite that never stopped. She poured out two glasses of wine instead. One for herself and one for Helen. Helen was determined not to accept it. She ended up knocking back two glasses. The wine took the edge off her voice. "My life is so mediocre," she said. She mumbled something else, poured herself another glass of wine, and walked down to the riverbank. She looked very small in Canyon's dress. She stayed by the river for the rest of the day, watching the dark water flow by.

Chapter Twenty-Seven

Helen threw out all the paper from the dining room. She said she had a lot of mind-clearing to do before she could start writing again. I made dinner: tuna sandwiches. We spent the rest of the evening in comfortable silence alone in our rooms.

The next morning Helen drove me down to the river. This time, Canyon made me swim next to the boat, which was even more dangerous than getting cramps. She almost ran me over *three* times. Never mind. I'd rather be run over than swim too far from the boat.

During that week, we all became changed women in a way. Helen was eating a lot more, Mrs. Canyon didn't eat as much, and I didn't think about Chester once. Well, maybe every now and then. I am also beginning to feel much stronger and safer in the water. By the end of the week, I had made it to the mouth of the river. I even swam a few metres into the Lake! That was some experience. Both terrifying and incredible. Here I am, Lake, I thought as I made those first strokes into it, I was really in it now. I don't know if it's possible for water to feel older, but this water did. I was swimming through centuries of water. Like entering a tomb of some pharaoh. I swam right out to the buoy,

Canyon called me back. That was enough for one day. She invited us to her place to celebrate. Seconds after stepping into the house. Helen had a sneezing fit. She was allergic to cats. Canyon and I had to round them all up and lock them into the guest/book room. The cats struck up a chorus of howling. Canyon threw in a big bag of catnip. The cats became stoned silent. Only the Siamese kept up his unearthly keening until Canyon threatened to cut his vocal cords.

We finally sat down for dinner. Under Canyon's hospitality, there was enough to feed the entire neighborhood. Three different meat courses, five different vegetables, pasta, rice salad. She told us that when she was a university student, she had a summer job as a cook in a lumber camp and never got over cooking large meals.

"That's where I met my husband," she said as she passed Helen another helping of pasta. "Well, I called him my husband, but we never married."

"Good for you. Marriage is the death of love," said Helen serving up a verbal tennis match. Is sat like a net in the middle.

"Don't blame it on marriage," countered Mrs. Canyon. "Blame it on yourself."

"Then why didn't you get married?" asked Helen.

"Because back then, I only thought of myself as a big fat girl who never had a boyfriend. And I was just so thrilled when some man finally paid attention to me that I didn't want to scare him off."

"So that's how you measure your worth, by some man paying attention to you?"

"I measure my worth by my ability to love myself."

"And do you?" asked Helen.

"Yes."

"Then come you're so fat?"

"Because I love food even more."

"That's only partly true. You want to be fat because you're trying to hide your true self."

"No, I love myself so much that I want to create even more of me." Canyon's infectious laughter made me laugh too.

Helen remained serious, "Obesity is not something to be laughed at."

"Neither is straightening your hair."

Helen picked up a knife and slammed the butt end of it on the table. "I'm no longer straightening my hair, as you can see for yourself! And no fucking white woman's gonna tell me what to do with my hair!"

Canyon didn't flinch. She just kept right on. "Then why keep it all tight to your scalp? That's trying to straighten it if you ask me."

I thought about ducking under the table.

Helen put down the knife and threw a hand of pasta in Canyon's face. "Fuck you, fatso!"

"And fuck you too, boney-ass."

They sounded like two women my age.

As calm as could be, Canyon picked up the bits of pasta and put them in her mouth. Helen wasn't about to let Canyons' indifference make her angrier. She even smiled like she had somehow claimed a victory.

"Where are you folks from?" asked Mrs. Canyon dumping more pasta onto Helen's plate.

Why was she giving Helen more ammunition?

"I was a foster child, just like Penny. Well, not just...like her." Helen's voice faltered a bit. She looked at me for some reaction. I remained pokerfaced. "I mean, unlike her, I stayed put in my foster home. My foster parents took very good care of me. They were white, of course, very liberal, very open-minded. It took them a long time to adopt me, of course, because they weren't sure how I would turn out. And, of course, I understand that because I was the only black child in a totally white neighborhood, so there was no telling how that might affect me. But I turned out to be the perfect child and teenager. I never caused them any trouble. I did everything right."

"What do all those 'of courses' mean?" asked Mrs. Canyon.

Having escaped from the lockup, two cats came through the open dining-room window, jumped on the table, and helped themselves to whatever caught their fancy.

Helen immediately started sneezing. That put a merciful end to the conversation and the dinner.

On the drive home, Helen asked me what had become of the man Mrs. Canyon had loved. I told her everything Canyon had told me. "She should not have sold the piano," Helen said. "Playing music or any kind of artistic endeavor gets us through pain more than anything else. That's what my foster parents told me."

"Did you really like them?" I asked.

"Like? I loved them. I loved them both very much, but I was like a trophy to them."

"A trophy?"

"Yes, to show how liberal they were. They always told me how grateful I should be about it not mattering to them that I was black. But if it didn't matter to them, why did they keeping saying it over and over again?"

"Because they were assholes."

"No," Her voice was quivering like tears were on their way. "They were good people."

We both remained silent for the rest of the way home.

When we pulled into the drive, Chester was sitting on the front porch.

Chapter Twenty-Eight

So much for my getting over Chester, I was thrilled to see him, and he was even sober. However, he wasn't waiting for me. He was looking for Dan.

"Dan doesn't live here anymore," said Helen. "Are you his long-lost son or something?"

"No, just a friend."

"Oh, I see," replied Helen even though she looked confused. "I have no idea where Dan is."

Did I need a cement wall to fall on me before I stopped this pathetic obsession with Chester? Yes, "I know where he is," I said. I told Chester the name of the motel and how to get there. "Mind if I come along?" I asked. "I'd like to see him too." Chester just shrugged. That was good enough for me. He headed for his car.

Helen tried to stop me. She didn't like the look of Chester. I told her Chester was dying of leukemia, and I was his only friend.

"You never told me she was black," Chester said before I could even get my seat belt buckled. "That must be strange."

"Yeah, she's strange all right," I replied, clicking in the seat belt," that's when it dawned on me that we weren't in Chester's car. "Whose car is this?"

"My old man's. He just kicked me out," he said as we rocketed out from the curb.

"How come?"

"I've been working my fucking ass off at fucking McDonald's. So, I take one fucking day off because it's my fucking birthday, and because of that, he decides that he won't put up half the fucking money for my fucking car. So I told him to take his fucking money and shove it up to his fucking ass. So he tells me to get out of the fucking house, so I did. Only I took his fucking car with me."

"You *stole* it?"

"Yeah, I was gonna dump it in the fucking lake. But I figured I needed a car to get out of his fucking life."

"I've gotten out of many people's lives without a car."

"It's different for girls. Next to jerking off, a car's the most important thing in a guy's life." He made a sharp right turn into the motel parking lot. We missed a head-on collision by an inch.

He parked the car and went into the motel check-in while I waited for my heart to start beating again.

Apparently, Dan had checked out about an hour ago. We started driving again, only this time it was a lot slower. We were traveling as much under the speed limit as we had gone over it before. Chester didn't react to anything I said. His jaw was set in a glum pout. He was lost in his own world, one that had no place for me.

When we stopped for a red light, I should have gotten out and never looked back. But I couldn't bring myself to do that. If I had to spend the rest of my life driving in a stolen car with him, never knowing where I'd end up, it would be worth it. It would be worth it even if he never spoke to me or listened to what I was saying, just sitting next to him was enough. What I had felt that morning swimming in the Lake didn't hold a candle to what I was feeling now.

We ended up on a street that looked very familiar. Lisa lived on this street. "What the hell is are you doing?" I screamed. He ignored me like I was invisible. He pulled into Lisa's driveway, got out, and headed for the doorway.

I knew then why people commit crimes of passion. They were driven by the same dark force that was building up inside of me.

I saw Lisa open the door. They talked for a few minutes, and then he went inside. I sat there planning how I was going to murder Chester. A little glint of metal caught my eye. It was the car keys dangling from the ignition. There was another way of getting back at Chester.

I turned on the ignition, put the gears in reverse, and slowly backed out of the driveway. It took me a while to straighten out the car once

I rolled out onto the road. Thank God no other cars were coming. I drove about as fast as I walked. I pushed down a little harder on the accelerator, a little too hard. The sudden speed made me panic. I swerved out to the other lane just when another car was approaching. I made a hard right over the sidewalk and into a tree. I lept out of the car before the other driver could reach me and took off down the street. I didn't stop running until I got home.

Helen was on the phone when I got in. She waved at me frantically and yelled into the receiver.

"Here she is. She's home!" Then she yelled at me. "Did you crash a car into a tree?"

"Um...

"Well, did you?" she screamed louder.

"It's not his car. It's his father's."

"His father's! Oh, my God – well, it doesn't matter whose car it was. Did you crash it into a tree?"

"I guess so."

"You guess so? Answer YES or NO!"

"Yes!" I screamed back at her.

"You almost killed Lisa's brother!"

"Lisa's brother?"

"Here." She shoved the receiver at me. "You talk to her! It's Lisa."

Lisa's voice was amazingly calm. "Don't worry, Penny. Tony's all right, but why were you___"

Suddenly I hear Chester's voice on the line. "You fucking bitch! You totaled my dad's car."

Then I heard Lisa shouting at Chester. "If you're going to call her that, you can leave right now!"

While this was going on, Helen was yelling in my other ear. "I told you not to go with him!"

Then I heard Lisa's voice come on again. "Penny, it's me again___

She was interrupted by her mother's voice, "Lemme talk ta her."

"Mother, *please* just go back to bed."

Then Helen screamed, "I can't take any more of this from you! I'm calling Mrs. Horshaw!"

Then Lisa's mother was on the line. "Hello, baby, how ya doin'? Know who this is?"

"Yes, it's Mrs. McIver."

"The editor?" Helen asked.

This was turning into a complete farce.

"Now, now now, I tole ya nunna that Mrs. Stuff." Came Dorothy's slur through the receiver. "I tole ya ta call me Dorothy from the Land of Oz. Now, for yer infermashun I'm not all us-set' bout the entire car thing. Tony tole me everythin' that happened, and as far as he's concerned, he's fine, unner-sand?"

"Yes."

By this time, Helen had left the room waving her arms and muttering incoherently,

"I dunno why you were drivin' that car, but as far as I'm concerned it don't matter, understand 'cause everythin' is fine, ess-sip that son of a bitch Chess-er wants ta live in this house, and I already have a one son of a bitch livin' here, which is mainly, namely, my husband which is one son of a bitch too many ___"

"MOTHER give me the phone now!" Lisa yelled from the background.

"Anyways, sweet dreams, kid 'en snappy landin's."

Lisa got back on the line, "I'm terribly sorry about that."

"I'm the one that should be sorry, Lisa,"

"No, it's all Chester's fault. It was terrible what he did. I had no idea you were out in the car and just to leave you alone like that – but he's in so much trouble now. I can't just throw him out. He needs my help."

"Lisa, you don't have to___ "

"Would you like to talk to Tony?"

Before I could complete what I wasn't sure how to complete, Tony got on the line. "Are you okay?" I asked.

"Sure," he said, "what about you?"

"I'm okay."

" I thought you were up north."

"I got a few days off. So I came home for awhile, but I wasn't expecting that kind of welcome."

"I'm really sorry about what happened. It was a really dumb thing to do. I could explain why I did it, but ...I mean... it's so complicated and everything and I___"

"That's okay. Just forget it."

I was beginning to like the sound of his voice. "Maybe I could take you to a movie or something to make up for it."

"Oh, you don't have to do that. I'd just like to talk."

"Okay." There was a long pause. I guess he was waiting for me to say when we would meet, but I wasn't sure yet if I really wanted to

"Do you want to talk to Lisa?"

"No, just tell her I'm really sorry and that I hope everything works out with her and...well, just tell her that I hope everything works out okay?

"Okay, good night."

"Good night." I put the receiver carefully back on the phone.

"Who was that you were talking to?" Helen asked. I didn't know how long she had been standing behind me.

"Lisa's brother."

"The one you almost killed?"

"Yeah."

"Well, by the sound of your conversation, it doesn't seem to matter too much to him."

"He's a nice guy,"

"Beware of nice guys. They'll steer you away from your one true love." She waited for a respectful pause so as not to sound too interested. "Did you see Dan?"

"No, he had checked out of the motel."

"Where did he go?"

"I don't know."

"He's probably living with that woman. He told me he was going to."

"He told you?"

"Yes, he called me the night I started writing and said he was thinking about moving in with her. Isn't it amazing how quickly men can leave one relationship and start another? Just like trading in a car."

"But he told me he didn't care about her."

"Did he tell you she was a hairdresser?" Helen burst into laughter which collapsed into tears. "He won't ever come back now," she cried so hard I thought she would break apart. She would not let me comfort her. She pushed me away, saying I needed to sleep. I told her I couldn't get to sleep with her crying. I sat down on the floor next to her.

Chapter Twenty-Nine

I woke up in my bed the next morning. How I got there, I'll never know. I was too big for Helen to carry me up the stairs. But maybe she was a lot stronger than I thought. I looked at the clock. It was 9:00 a.m. The alarm hadn't gone off.

"I thought you needed some extra sleep," came Helen's voice from the doorway. Lisa was standing next to her,

"We've been waiting for you to wake up," said Lisa. "I insisted that Chester apologize for what he did last night. He's here too."

"What!" I screamed. This was all too much to take in seconds after waking up.

"Here," said Helen, handing me a bathrobe. "You'd better put this on."

"Ready?" asked Lisa.

"No."

Helen stepped aside to let Chester come into the room. Does anyone else have a life like mine?

Chester mumbled an apology, never looking me in the eye. It was all over in a few seconds. He nearly tripped over himself getting out the door. Helen went with him.

I felt like I was about to get over chronic constipation, which doesn't sound very poetic, but that's what it felt like. My yearning was about to be exorcised. It would never return. He would always be in love with Lisa, and that was the end of it. Really.

"Chester's going to say with us for a while," said Lisa "Until he gets this thing sorted out with his father. We're both going over there now to try and sort that thing out."

"You're amazing."

"No, I'm not. I'm just very responsible. And I felt so bad about what happened to you. I mean, when something bad happens to someone, it goes on and on. You were treated badly, so you got into the car and almost killed yourself and my brother, who got fired because___

"He was fired?"

"Yes."

"Why didn't he tell me that?"

"He was too embarrassed to."

"Oh, shit. He's fired, and then I almost crash a car into him."

"But you didn't. I mean, that's the important thing. I'm sure he'll get another job somewhere else."

"Why was he fired?"

"He got into a fight."

"Tony got into a fight?"

We were interrupted by Chester yelling up to my window, "Lisa, hurry up."

"I really shouldn't keep him waiting," said Lisa. "He's very anxious about talking to his father. I just wanted to say again that I wish you every success with your swim."

"Thanks," I replied.

"Do you have a date set?"

"A date?"

"When you're going to do it."

"Tomorrow."

"Tomorrow!"

"Yeah"

"Where are you going to start?"

"At the exact spot where Marilyn Bell finished her swim."

"Oh, that's wonderful. That's just wonderful. I'll be there to see you off."

She ran over to me, gave me a quick hug, and left to look after Chester.

Well, there I was, No more fooling around. I had made my date with destiny, which sounds pretty dramatic. But it was a pretty dramatic thing to do, to just say "tomorrow" like that, without consulting Mrs. Canyon, and with any hope in hell of actually doing it.

Chapter Thirty

Helen drove slowly past this beauty salon called Cuts' n' Curls on our way to the river. Dan's van was parked outside it. Through the salon's window, I saw Dan cutting a woman's hair. I caught only a glimpse of the woman. She looked a lot like Marilyn. No, that would be just too coincidental. I waved anyway.

"Don't wave," said Helen.

"I wasn't waving at Dan," I said.

"Who were you waving at?"

"I think it was someone I met once and was destined to see again."

"How can you live with someone for ten years and never really know them?" she said more to herself than to me. "I hope he's happy and – No, I don't. I hope he lives a life of constant misery."

"I'm going to swim Lake Ontario tomorrow."

"Tomorrow! But that's way too soon! You're not ready."

"Helen, we both know that I'll never be ready, but I can't wait anymore to see how far I get."

She just nodded in silent agreement.

When we arrived at the river, Mrs. Canyon was with a man who had a couple of front teeth missing, but that just added to his charm.

"Penny, Helen, this is Bob MacDougall, "said Mrs. Canyon. "He was a friend of my husband's. He owns the little outboard we've been using, but he says there's no way it could take on the Lake if it gets rough out there. So, he's going to let us use his bigger boat."

"She's a fifteen-meter cabin cruiser," Bob said, tipping his hat. "I'd be more 'en pleased ta escort you across the Lake in her."

"Penny's not ready to cross it yet," said Mrs. Canyon. "But she will be ready____

"Tomorrow," I said.

"Right," replied Mrs. Canyon, without any hint of a challenge. "Tomorrow's is good as any other day, I suppose."

"Well, let's see how ya swim," said Bob.

Canyon's boat was too small for all three of them, so Bob decided just to accompany me down the river. He was much more adept at keeping the boat on an even course. I swam along next to it without any fear, with even strokes. My confidence grew with each stroke.

However, it became apparent that Bob was more interested in telling me his story than watching me swim. It finally occurred to him that I couldn't hear him through my swimming cap or over the noise of the motor. So, he cut the engine, and I was forced to stop and listen.

"It's a good thing you're doing his," he said, "'course if you weren't swimming the Lake, then she wouldn't need ta use my boat. Ever since Harry died, I've been after her ta see me, only she won't have nuthin' ta do with me. Says she's still mournin'. Jeezus, it's been ten years since he died. I don't call that mournin'. I call that, bein' just plain stubborn. So's outta the blue she calls me up and asks ta use one of my boats. 'Sure, I say,' and how 'bout a little dinner ta go with it?' She says she'll go for the dinner but no hanky-panky. I says, 'Darlin' ya knows I've always been a gennelman.' So we goes out for dinner and little by little I can see that big old block of ice startin' ta melt a little. It isn't much, but it's a start. So as far as I'm concerned, ya can take as long as ya want swiminin' the Lake."

Chapter Thirty-One

Helen wasn't ever going to drive past Dan's beauty salon again. I would see him on my own. I would also phone Tony.

Lisa answered when I called. She told me that Chester's dad told her that he could come home as long as Chester was going out with her. I guess he thought Lisa could keep Chester on the straight and narrow. She was delighted when I asked to speak to Tony,

"Hi, again," I said when Tony got on the phone.

"Hi, how's it going?"

"Okay, I just wanted to tell you that I'm going to swim Lake Ontario tomorrow."

"Yeah," Lisa told me.

There was a pause, and then the something clicked on inside both of us. We laughed. In fact, I'd never laughed so hard in my life. "So, still want to get together to talk?" I asked.

"Yeah, I'll come over around eight, Okay?"

"Okay," I said, and that was that.

After I hung up, I looked through the Yellow Pages for the number of Cuts n Curls. A woman answered, and I knew just by her "Good evening, Cut's n Curls," that it was the same woman who had been with Dan in the van. I just couldn't tell her straight out who I was, so I made an appointment to get my hair cut. She said she had an opening at six with a new stylist. I asked his name, and she said Dan. I told her my name was Colette.

The woman behind the reception desk at Cuts n Curls could have modeled for a Dresden figurine. She had porcelain skin, light blue eyes, and very blond hair, now loose over her shoulders in soft waves. She was the exact opposite of Helen. "Dan just stepped out, but he'll be back in a few minutes," she said. "I'll wash your hair in the meantime."

Maybe she did recognize me because her fingers dug into my scalp like claws. "If you don't mind me saying. I think your hair needs a lot of conditioner."

"I've been swimming a lot," I explained.

"Chlorine ain't good for your hair."

Helen would never have used "ain't," I would tell Helen. It might make her feel superior. No, it wouldn't

"Have a date tonight?" she asked, squeezing out half a bottle of conditioner onto my head.

"Sort of."

"A pretty girl like you must have a lot of dates."

Pretty? No way I was pretty. She was just buttering me up like she would any customer.

Dan came in just as she was wrapping up my wet hair in a towel, "I gotta customer for you."

"Penny?" Dan looked at me as if I were a ghost.

"No, it's Colette," said the woman.

"No, it's Penny," I said.

"Penny?" The woman looked more pissed off than surprised. "You're Penny?"

Dan and I both answered, yes.

"You came here to spy for Helen. What a little shit you are!"

"Yeah, I'm a shit, but Helen doesn't know I'm here. I just wanted to see Dan."

"You could have just said that on the phone. But you wanted to check me out first, didn't cha." She lit up a cigarette.

"Honey, we're not supposed to smoke in here," said Dan. The *honey* came out with real easy affection. Helen would just die if she knew that.

"So, arrest me."

Dan was caught between two women again.

"It's okay, Dan," I said. "I'll just go."

"No, say what you want to say to him," the woman said, walking to the exit door. "I'm goin' for a coffee."

"You don't have to go anywhere," I replied.

"Don't worry, sweetie, I ain't going 'anywhere for long," she said, pushing open the door with a hard thrust. Dan must have a thing for tough women.

"She'll be all right," said Dan after she had left.

"You're always saying that about women."

"What else can a guy like me say about them?"

"Who is a guy like you?"

"Just regular, I guess."

"No, you're exceptional."

"It's good to see you, Penny. How you been doin?"

"Okay."

"How's Helen?"

"She's fine. I mean for being Helen, she's fine."

"I had no other choice but to leave, you know. She wanted me out. And now ...well, now you can see for yourself, I'm doin' what I' m supposed to be doin.'"

"If what's-her-name didn't____"

"Her name is Bev, believe it or not."

"You're kidding? Well, if Bev didn't own a beauty salon, would you still be with her?"

"If Helen hadn't kicked me out, I wouldn't've met her. And well, she needs me more than Helen does."

"Do you love her?"

"I'm sure in time I will."

"So you're still in love with Helen?"

"I'll always be in love with Helen, but she doesn't love me. I don't think Helen is capable of loving anyone."

"Yes, she is. But I'm not."

"Yes, you are. You'll see."

"I'm going to swim the Lake tomorrow. I think I've dragged this crazy thing out a lot longer than is necessary. I might as well get it over with."

"I'll be there to see you off."

I told him where I would start my swim, said goodbye, and shared a little hug. Then he asked me if I still wanted my haircut. I told him I'd be back some other time.

Tony was waiting on the porch when I got home. We went for a walk, and we ended up at the park where we first met.

Chapter Thirty-Two

There was a thunderstorm brewing. The wind had already started up. The branches of an old oak next to our picnic table creaked and groaned as they swayed over us. It wasn't the safest place to be, but I somehow felt immune to danger sitting next to Tony.

"I have something for you," he said, digging into his pocket. "I kept it for a special occasion, and I think the night before you swim Lake Ontario is special enough. I found your grandmother's ring." He handed me a black plastic Batman ring.

I accepted it like it was made of gold.

"I stole it when I was nine years old, but I was too afraid to wear it." His laughter was so graceful and pure.

The wind was really whipping up the branches above us. Lightning cracked. The scene was set for raw sex. We would make out right there on the table, and lighting would hit the tree, we would be crushed by it and die in each other's arms.

"You looked so lost that night I first saw you," he said. "I know how that feels."

"Well, I haven't exactly been found yet," I said I wanted him to kiss me so badly. There was a pain in my groin. I'd never had the pain before, even with Chester. I couldn't look at him. He would see it, and I wanted him so badly.

"At first, I thought you were a serial killer," I added Oh, what a dumb thing to say. He would be completely turned off.

"That's funny. I thought you were one too." We both laughed.

I would look at him. I would look at him right now, and then he would see it and then___

"What's your favorite colour?" he asked.

"Red."

"Who's your favorite singer?"

"Freddie Mercury."

"That's incredible. He's mine too."

I was looking at him now. He must be able to see it. I could tell by his eyes that he was feeling something too.

"What's your favorite movie?"

Please don't' ask any more questions. Just do it. Just take me.

"Mine's *Death in Venice,*" he continued.

Why doesn't he get off this question thing I wondered. I was in love with him. And this time, it would be a real, true, shining love.

"Do you believe there are many different kinds of love?" he asked.

"Yeah, but there's only one that counts. The one true love."

"Every love has truth to it. Every love counts."

What I had been waiting for finally happened.

He kissed me. The kiss ended quickly. I wanted more and more of it. I pulled him closer to me and kissed him harder. But he wasn't really kissing me back I mean, there wasn't any passion to it. It was horrifying,

"I love you, Penny, but I'm...gay."

Chapter Thirty-Three

That was the biggest joke anyone had ever played on me. It was just too funny. What did you expect, Penny Maybe? You and all the fuckin "maybes" in your life. Well, there will be no more maybes. No one will ever find me here. And where's here? Here is under what remains of me and an abandoned boat somewhere along the shore of the Lake. It's crazy out there. The waves are so high they could hit this boat any minute now and swallow us both up. How the hell did I get here? I can see two legs stand outside of the boat. They're Tony's legs.

"Come on, Penny, let's go."

"Fuck you."

Tony brought me here. How did that happen?

"Get lost, you fucking faggot." That would do it. He would really hate me now. He would leave and take his two skinny lets with him. The legs remained. How many more people would I need to hate before my life was over? My throat felt sore. I must have done a lot of screaming.

"Come on, Penny, you need to get home."

Home? I had no home. I had nothing. No one. There was a little voice inside me that knew that was wrong. *You have me*, it said.

Tony moved away from the boat. I could stay with all this hate, or I could listen to that little voice.

Chapter Thirty-Four

I am standing on the shore of Lake Ontario. The sky is clear, and the water is calm. Mrs. Canyon, Helen, Dan, Lisa, and Tony are out on Bob MacDougall's boat waiting for me to start my swim. Chester would be here too, but he had to work.

I step into the Lake.

About the Author

Kathleen Martin's first novel "Penny Maybe" was published in Canada and in Germany. She is also a Gemini-nominated writer for film and an award-winning playwright. She lives in Phoenix, Arizona.

Read more at https://www.facebook.com/KathleenMartinauthor.